This book belongs to

....

The activities and recipes within this book are for the family to enjoy doing together.
Some could be dangerous without the help of an adult. Children, please have an adult
with you when you are using scissors and knives, or handling anything hot.

You can find beautiful wild flowers growing in fields, gardens and hedgerows.
It is far better not to pick them, but to leave them to bloom in their own special places.

A YEAR OF STORIES AND THINGS TO DO
A BODLEY HEAD BOOK 978 0 370 33248 2

Published in Great Britain by The Bodley Head,
an imprint of Random House Children's Publishers UK
A Random House Group Company

This edition published 2014

1 3 5 7 9 10 8 6 4 2

Copyright © Shirley Hughes, 2014

ELLA'S BIG CHANCE © Shirley Hughes, 2003
DON'T WANT TO GO! © Shirley Hughes, 2010
A JOURNEY TO THE NORTH POLE and ALFIE UPSTREAM from *Alfie Weather* © Shirley Hughes, 2001
LOST SHEEP and ALFIE GOES CAMPING from *The Big Alfie Out of Doors Storybook* © Shirley Hughes, 1992
ALFIE'S FEET © Shirley Hughes, 1982
THE GARDEN PATH, ONE WINTER EVENING and SUMMER NUMBERS from *Rhymes for Annie Rose* © Shirley Hughes, 1995
LOOKING FOR WINNIE from *Alfie's World* © Shirley Hughes, 2006
JONADAB AND RITA © Shirley Hughes, 2008
WHERE'S ALFIE?, THE VERY SPECIAL BIRTHDAY and GOOSE WEATHER from *All About Alfie* © Shirley Hughes, 2011
BOBBO GOES TO SCHOOL © Shirley Hughes, 2012
ALFIE WINS A PRIZE © Shirley Hughes, 2004
LATE SONG and A MIDWINTER'S NIGHT DREAM from *Stories by Firelight* © Shirley Hughes, 1993
All first published in Great Britain by The Bodley Head.

The right of Shirley Hughes to be identified as the author of this work has been
asserted in accordance with the Copyright, Designs and Patents Act 1988.

The Random House Group Limited supports the Forest Stewardship Council® (FSC®), the leading international
forest-certification organisation. Our books carrying the FSC label are printed on FSC®-certified paper. FSC is
the only forest-certification scheme supported by the leading environmental organisations, including Greenpeace.
Our paper procurement policy can be found at www.randomhouse.co.uk/environment

RANDOM HOUSE CHILDREN'S PUBLISHERS UK
61–63 Uxbridge Road, London W5 5SA

www.randomhousechildrens.co.uk
www.randomhouse.co.uk

Addresses for companies within The Random House Group Limited can be found at: www.randomhouse.co.uk/offices.htm

THE RANDOM HOUSE GROUP Limited Reg. No. 954009

A CIP catalogue record for this book is available from the British Library.

Printed and bound in China

A YEAR OF
STORIES

AND THINGS TO DO

Shirley Hughes

THE BODLEY HEAD
LONDON

Contents

For Fiona Macmillan

With thanks to
Andrea MacDonald

Every month has its very own
special flower for you to try and spot.
You can find beautiful wild flowers
growing in fields, gardens and hedgerows.
It is far better not to pick them, but to leave
them to bloom in their own special places.

Welcome to

A YEAR OF
STORIES
AND THINGS TO DO

This collection of seasonal stories and things to do is the kind of book I would like to have come across in my own childhood. I grew up in a pre-television, pre-computer era when there seemed to be acres of time to fill in. We combated boredom as best we could. My sister and I were forever dressing up and trying to act plays, bursting out from behind the sitting-room curtains, hoping for applause.

I drew a lot, made paper dolls and designed their clothes, and tried to write and illustrate stories. I even started a magazine. I was not only the editor but its sole contributor. It was called *Girls Own* and featured a trio of schoolgirls called "the Wreckless Three." Also a serial story which ended, excitingly: "to be continued in our next edition." The magazine folded after the first edition, but I enjoyed giving it a try.

This is a book which I hope will not only offer stories and pictures for all seasons, but also maybe encourage readers to dream up some of their own ideas, try their hand at new skills and get out and about. It is endlessly interesting out there, and fabulously beautiful too, whatever the time of year.

Shirley Hughes x

Snowdrop

*Snowdrops are one of the earliest bulbs to
flower and can be found in damp woods,
meadows, shady gardens or beside streams.
Their name is taken from their delicate
white blooms that resemble little droplets.*

January

Christmas is over, but there's lots to celebrate in the New Year. If it's cold outside there's plenty to do indoors.

On Twelfth Night it's time to take down the Christmas tree and put away all the sparkly decorations until next year, but it's an excellent time to dress up, and perhaps put on a show of your own. You could make a programme and some cakes to hand round in the interval. Find out more after reading *Ella's Big Chance*.

Ella's Big Chance

Mr Cinders kept a little dress shop in a quiet but elegant part of town.

People came from far and near to buy clothes from him because he made such lovely things.

His wife had died, leaving him with one daughter, a red-haired girl called Ella whom he dearly loved. He taught her about silks and wools and satins and how to coax them into coats and dresses. So, by and by, she became as good a dressmaker as he was, if not better.

Mr Cinders and Ella ran the shop together with the help of a lively lad called Buttons. This was his name because he wore a short jacket with three rows of shiny buttons on the front. He also wore trousers with a gold stripe down the sides and a round cap set on at a jaunty angle.

Buttons polished the glass on the front of the shop until it shone, and opened the door for the customers. In the afternoon he bicycled about the town delivering parcels and boxes.

In between times, whenever he could, he would chat to Ella while she was busy sewing. He could always make her laugh, even if her mouth was full of pins.

All went on happily until the terrible day when Mr Cinders decided to marry again. His new wife seemed to pop up from nowhere like a sharp-eyed, expensively dressed jack-in-the-box. Still worse, she had two daughters of her own, and very beautiful creatures they were too.

Madame Renée was her name and she soon changed things at the shop. She had everything redecorated and enlarged the salon. She put advertisements in all the smart magazines to increase trade. This meant that Ella and her father and Buttons had to work harder than ever.

Neither Madame Renée nor her daughters knew how to sew. Instead, Madame Renée managed everything and her two daughters, Ruby and Pearl, were models.

They strolled languidly up and down, showing off the clothes to the customers.

The shop was now a huge success, and all might have been well if Ruby and Pearl had not behaved so spitefully to Ella. They called her names like Podge and Carrots and expected her to wait on them as they lazed about on cushioned divans.

They kept Ella working such long hours at her sewing machine that she hardly had a moment to herself. If she fell asleep at the workroom table they woke her up and scolded her. Now she no longer had a room of her own. She shared a cramped basement full of cuttings and rolls of cloth with the old grey cat.

Mr Cinders was far too much under his wife's thumb to interfere. Ella could tell by his face that he knew things were going badly wrong. But he seemed suddenly to have grown old and could only remain silent as his stepdaughters preened themselves in the beautiful gowns which Ella had made, while the only thing she, his own daughter, had to wear was a shabby black dress.

The one person who took Ella's side was loyal Buttons. These days he hated working at the shop but he stayed in the job for her sake. He often exchanged sharp words with Ruby and Pearl when Madame Renée was out of earshot. Privately he called them a couple of puffed-up, dressed-up, made-up, stuck-up, brainless parakeets.

Whenever he could, he would slip down to Ella's basement and try to cheer her up. He would strum his guitar and coaxed her to sing the songs that reminded them of happier times.

Sometimes they even danced together, two little figures in the moonlit room, moving softly in and out among the bales of cloth.

The most important customer who came to the shop was the Duchess of Arc, a lady of enormous wealth. She always arrived in her luxurious car and swept into the salon, swathed in furs and superb diamonds.

Then how Madame Renée fussed and flattered and commanded Ruby and Pearl to parade all the best gowns that Ella's clever fingers had created.

Imagine the excitement when one day an invitation arrived from the Duchess announcing that a grand ball was to be held at her villa in honour of her only son, the Duke of Arc, lately returned from abroad. All the ladies and gentlemen of any importance in the neighbourhood were asked to attend.

At once Ruby and Pearl began to vie with one another in a very jealous manner about what they intended to wear.

The shop was thrown into a fever of activity. There was such a posturing in front of mirrors and draping of silks and satins, such a confusion of feathers and jewellery, that the place began to look like an Aladdin's cave. Ella was set to work night and day to make their dresses, and a very good job she made of it.

"Will I be going to the ball too?" she asked when every last stitch was finished to perfection. Ruby and Pearl merely sniggered rudely at this.

"You? Go to the ball?" they said. "No chance, Carrots, you're far too shabby. Besides, you couldn't possibly get into any of the dresses!"

"I think you're mean!" cried Ella. "The invitation was for all of us!"

"Good heavens, child, surely you can understand that it would never do for us to be seen with someone like you!" was all they replied.

Ella was too proud to cry.

On the evening of the ball
she helped them to arrange their
hair and put on their dresses,
pretending that she didn't care.
When at last the hired limousine
arrived, Ruby, in shades of red,
Pearl, in palest pink, and
Madame Renée, all a-glitter in
black, swept out without even
saying goodbye.

Only Mr Cinders lingered for
a moment to kiss his daughter
goodnight with a sad look which
said: "You see how it is. There's
nothing I can do."

Then they were gone.

Ella went slowly downstairs
to her dreary basement room and
sat down on the floor among the
snippets of cloth. She gathered
the old grey cat onto her lap.
"I'll bet it's a horrible stuck-up
affair anyway," she whispered.
"But, oh, puss, I would love to
have seen it all!" And a few hot
tears fell onto his fur.

Just then there came a soft
tap on the door and there was
Buttons.

"So they wouldn't let you go,
Ella," he said. 'Downright
spiteful, I call it. You're twice
as pretty as they are. But never
mind. I'm cooking bacon and
eggs in the kitchen. Come on,
we'll have a party of our own."

In the kitchen Buttons put
on an apron and got busy at the
stove while Ella fetched the milk
from the doorstep.

Just as she stepped out a
strange lady stepped in, carrying
a fancy umbrella.

"I am your Fairy Godmother,"
she told Ella, briskly peeling
off her gloves. "It's my job to
see that you go to the ball, so
don't let's waste time. First,
I must think how to get you there.
Come outside, both of you, and
bring the cat."

Outside in the street the
Fairy Godmother looked about
her thoughtfully. There was
nothing in sight which looked
very promising as transport –
only Buttons' old delivery
bicycle which was propped up
against the railings. But when
the Fairy Godmother tapped it
lightly with her folded umbrella
it instantly turned into a large,
grey, gleaming limousine.

Then just another tap on the
old cat's head transformed him
at once into a smart chauffeur,
dressed in an immaculate
dove-grey uniform, who stood
by the open door.

Ella clasped Buttons' hand tightly in amazement.

"But I can't go to the ball," she cried. 'Not like this. I look terrible.'

The Fairy Godmother sketched a shape in the air with her umbrella and at once Ella was dressed in a ball dress as light as a silver cobweb, glittering all over with crystal beads, which fitted her perfectly. She wore a tiny silk hat to hide her hair in case she was recognized, silver stockings and – tap! tap! – a pair of little glass slippers on her feet.

"Oh, Ella!" was all Buttons could say. He had never seen her look so elegant.

"You are to be home by the last stroke of midnight," the Fairy Godmother told Ella. "The magic only lasts until then. After that it's back to normal."

"I won't forget," cried Ella excitedly as she stepped into the car.

"Enjoy yourself, Ella!" Buttons called after her as she was driven away. Ella waved from the back window of the car until she was out of sight.

When Buttons looked round, the Fairy Godmother seemed to have gone too. "Now there's nobody left to share the bacon and eggs, not even the cat," he said aloud. And he went back, all alone, into the shop.

Ella caused quite a stir when she arrived at the ball. None of the guests had seen such a striking girl before or one who was so beautifully dressed. And when the Duchess of Arc herself presented Ella to her son, gossip rustled around the ballroom like a hot wind through dry grass. But nobody, not even Ella's family, guessed who she was.

The Duke was dark-haired, grey-eyed and very, very handsome. He asked Ella to dance and they took the floor. All the other guests fell away.

Ella found she was not in the least over-awed by him. They chatted and laughed as they glided and spun, two-stepped, quick-stepped, fox-trotted and tangoed in perfect time together.

In the supper room, lit by a hundred paper lanterns, the Duke had eyes only for her.

He had never met a girl like her. She was so full of life, so ready to enjoy herself, compared with the cool, languid beauties of his own circle.

Of course, Ella did not notice the time. Why should she? She was having too much fun. She was waltzing in the Duke's arms when the clock began to strike midnight. What a terrible shock for Ella!

One . . .

    two . . .

        three . . .

"I've got to go!" she muttered, diving across the ballroom and scattering the astonished dancers.

Four . . . five . . . six . . .

She ran out of the French windows and down the many marble steps to the garden below.

"Stay, stay with me a moment!" cried the Duke, hurrying after her. But Ella was fleeing away into the darkness.

Seven . . . eight . . . nine . . .

"I don't even know your name!" he called. All he heard was the faint clang of the iron gates as they closed behind her.

On the steps, at his feet, lay a little glass slipper.

Ten . . . eleven . . . twelve!

The last stroke came just as Ella reached the big grey limousine with the chauffeur holding wide the door. In an instant all that remained was Buttons' battered bicycle lying in the middle of the road. Beside it was the old grey cat with his coat standing on end, looking extremely put out.

Ella looked down at her black dress. It seemed shabbier than ever. But somehow she found she was holding in her hand one little glass slipper.

She put it into her pocket and picked up the bicycle. Sadly, she had never learned to ride one so she had to push it all the way back to the shop, limping along the road in her bare feet.

The cat, refusing a lift in the basket, stalked off crossly into the night to make his own way home.

The next day Ruby and Pearl did not bother to get out of bed until the afternoon, when they finally appeared, sluggish and sulky. They settled down over coffee to gossip about the ball. Who was the mysterious beauty who had so fascinated the Duke? Though they would never have admitted it, they were seething with jealousy.

Ella said nothing. Instead she slipped down to her basement room and took the little glass slipper from its hiding place under a pile of old scraps. She simply did not know what to make of it all.

Meanwhile the Duke wandered
restlessly through the gardens of the
villa. He looked at the glass slipper
and sighed. He had been accustomed
to the company of the most charming
ladies in Europe but none had touched
his heart like the stranger who had so
enchanted him at the ball.

"I must find her!" he whispered.

Right away he set out to search for
the girl who had worn the glass slipper.
He visited every street, every house in
town. But wherever he went, no lady's
foot quite fitted. He began to despair.

Finally he arrived at Mr Cinders'
dress shop. Madame Renée and her
daughters were all agog to receive
such a distinguished guest. When he
explained his visit Ruby and Pearl
quite forgot themselves and pushed
forward eagerly, jostling one another
in a very undignified manner.

With a great deal of fuss and
bother and fluttering of eyelashes
they vied to try on the glass slipper,
first Ruby, then Pearl. But though
they both pushed and shoved and
pleaded and squashed up their
toes, it was no use. The slipper
simply did not fit.

Madame Renée, who had
been peering intently over their
shoulders like a beady-eyed
blackbird trying to capture a
worm, could hardly contain her
rage and disappointment.

The Duke prepared to leave.
Then he noticed a figure standing
in the shadows. A servant, surely,
he thought, judging by her shabby
dress, though there was something
about her, something familiar.

"Will you try it?"' he asked.
The others snorted in amusement.
Slowly Ella came forward and
sat down.

Of course, the slipper
fitted her foot perfectly. There
was a gasp of astonishment.
And when Ella produced the
other matching slipper from
her pocket even Madame Renée
was stunned into silence.

The Duke took Ella's hand.
"I was afraid I might never see
you again," he said. "But now
I have found you I cannot let
you go. Come away with me at
once and we will announce our
engagement!"

Ella looked around. She saw
that her stepsisters' faces were
ugly with envy and bad temper.
She had not noticed Buttons.
In fact, she had not noticed him
at all recently because she had
been so taken up with the glories
of the ball. But she noticed him
now.

He was hovering in a corner,
pretending to be busy tying up
a brown paper parcel.

"No,'" said Ella slowly.
"Thank you very much, Duke,
but no. I'm sorry – I can't. You
see, I love someone else."

At that moment Buttons
looked up at her. And a bright
pink blush of hope spread up all
over his face to the very tips
of his ears.

Mr Cinders started to smile for the first time in a long while. And when his wife pinched his arm crossly and hissed, "Do something!" he merely smiled wider than ever.

Madame Renée took the Duke aside and said, "Why not consider one of my daughters instead, your grace? Utterly charming, I'm sure you'll agree. And a better class of girl altogether!"

But the Duke shook his head politely and hurried away from the house as fast as he could. Soon, it was rumoured, he had taken off in his private aeroplane to explore the South American jungle and recover from his broken heart.

"You could have been very rich, you know," Buttons said to Ella when they were alone together at last.

"Dear Buttons, I don't fancy being a grand lady. I just want to be with you," she replied. "And anyway, it could get a bit dull doing nothing all day except being dressed up like an expensive doll. We'll go off and start our own little shop and I'll make stunning clothes, more beautiful than anyone has ever seen. And what's more," she added, "I'll have first pick of them."

"When we are married," said Buttons, "you may not live like a duchess but you will eat like a queen. You never did try my bacon and eggs, did you?"

So off they went, with Ella
on the crossbar of the bicycle,
wobbling a bit because they were
laughing so much, and the old grey
cat in the basket. It was a lot more
fun than being in the back of a
limousine.

They were too happy to notice
a lady walking alone further up
the street, carrying a fancy
umbrella. She paused to watch
them go. Then, smiling a secret
smile, she walked on.

Things to do in January

Putting on a show

People often go to see pantomimes around Christmas time and in January. You could put on your own show, based on a story you know well. *Ella's Big Chance* is based on the story of *Cinderella*, but set in a different time. You could use this, or another traditional story like *Jack and the Beanstalk*, *Puss in Boots*, *Aladdin* or *Dick Whittington*.

- Once you've picked your story, you need to decide on your script. If it's a story you know well, you can make up your own words.

- Who is going to be in your play? Make a list of characters and decide who is going to play them.

- Now you need somewhere to perform the show. Characters have to come on and off stage, and you need somewhere for your audience to sit.

- How will your stage be lit? Will the audience be sitting in the dark?

- Costumes and props can help you get into character. What props do you need for your story? You can make simple ones out of paper – for instance, folding paper into a concertina to make a fan, or rolling it into a cone and securing with sticky tape to make a megaphone.

- How can you dress up like your character? Dressing gowns can be useful, as well as towels, scarves and anything sparkly. Perhaps you can make a crown or a hat using paper and cardboard, measuring around your head, then stapling it together and decorating.

- Will there be songs, music or dancing in your show? Perhaps some of your cast can play instruments, do gymnastic tricks, juggle or tell jokes.

- Now you need to make a poster advertising your show, and even tickets for your audience.

Have fun putting on your show and make sure you all bow or curtsey at the end when your audience applauds!

Puppets

Another way of putting on a show is by using puppets. This might be a good idea if you haven't got many cast members. You can make simple finger puppets with decorated paper. If you have an old glove, or one that has lost its partner, you can ask if you can cut off the fingers and decorate them with glue, wool and anything you like to make a face. Or you can make sock puppets by gluing coloured paper, buttons and wool onto old socks.

Fun with wool

When it's cold outside, it's fun to make things indoors. Do you know how to knit or crochet? All you need are two knitting needles or a crochet hook, some wool and an adult to help you. Or, to start with, you can try finger-knitting – looping the wool around your fingers to make a chain. There are lots of things you can make with wool: tying bows or tassels, braiding into plaits to make bracelets, or making pom-poms.

Resolutions and diaries

Many people make New Year's resolutions in January. They think of things they would like to achieve in the coming year. What would you like to do this year? Are there any new things you'd like to try?

January can be a good time to start a diary, so you can remember all the things that happen throughout the year.

Did you know . . . ?

In some parts of Great Britain people take part in a traditional ceremony called wassailing in January: they sing to the trees to help keep them healthy.

Crocus

*Crocuses are goblet-shaped flowers,
usually purple, yellow or white.
Many have strong perfumes that
lure bees out of their hives.*

February

It's great to get a card or letter through the post. I specially love the ones I get from readers who have enjoyed my books and tell me which bits they like best. Sometimes they have even included a drawing or story of their own.

In February you can make a Valentine card to send to someone you love, or a special box, or even a decorated matchbox with some tiny surprises inside. There are more ideas in my story *Don't Want to Go!*

Don't Want to Go!

One morning, Lily's mum did
not want to get up. She just
lay there with her eyes closed.
She said that her head ached
and her throat was sore and
she felt hot and shivery all over.

"Mum has got flu, I'm afraid," Dad said as he gave Lily her breakfast. "She needs to stay in bed today and I have to go to work." He looked worried.

"Who will look after me, then?" Lily wanted to know.

Dad was already speaking on the phone. When he rang off he said, "Guess what! You're going to play at Melanie's house! Won't that be fun?"

"Who's Melanie?" asked Lily.

"You remember Melanie! You've been to her house before. She lives just near here in Wesley Avenue and she has a big boy called Jack and a baby called Sam!"

"I've dropped the yellow bit of my egg on the floor," was all Lily said.

"There'll be lots of nice toys to play with,"
Dad said. He wiped Lily's mouth and mopped
the floor. Then he buttoned her into her jacket and
put on her hat and mittens.

"Don't want to go!" said Lily.

"I'll take you in the buggy, it will be quicker,"
said Dad as he tucked Bobbo in beside her.

"Off we go!" he said in a very jolly voice.
They were just turning into Wesley Avenue
when Dad discovered that Lily's mittens were gone.

"I'm sure we put them on before we left the
house," he said.

He turned the buggy round.

They were halfway home before they found
the mittens lying on the pavement.

Dad picked them up and put them safely
back on Lily's hands again. Then he pushed
the buggy full steam ahead till they reached
Melanie's front door.

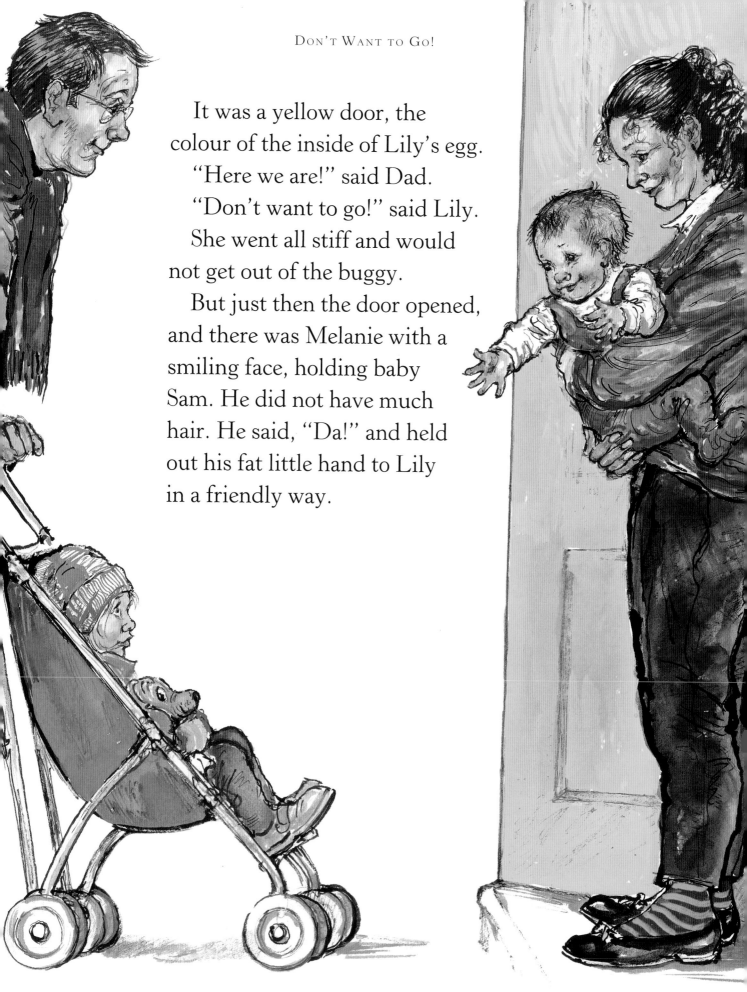

It was a yellow door, the colour of the inside of Lily's egg.

"Here we are!" said Dad.

"Don't want to go!" said Lily.

She went all stiff and would not get out of the buggy.

But just then the door opened, and there was Melanie with a smiling face, holding baby Sam. He did not have much hair. He said, "Da!" and held out his fat little hand to Lily in a friendly way.

Lily and Dad stepped into Melanie's hall. Lily was clutching Bobbo very tightly. Dad knelt down. He took off Lily's hat and mittens and gave her a big hug. "Have a good time, darling," he said. "I'll finish work early."

"Don't want to stay," said Lily in a tiny voice.

As the door closed on Dad, Lily opened her mouth
to give a big yell. But at that moment a little dog ran into
the hall. He was white with pale brown ears and patches.
He ran straight up to Lily and licked her hand.

Lily liked that. She decided not to yell for the moment
after all.

"His name's Ringo," Melanie
told her. "And it looks as though
he likes you a lot."

They all went into the kitchen. It was warm in there. Ringo's basket was in the corner.

Melanie put Sam in his highchair. "Sam's going to have some toast and honey. Would you like some?" she asked.

"Don't want toast," said Lily. She forgot to say thank you.

While Sam sat in his chair and ate toast and honey, Lily and Bobbo sat under the table.

When Sam had finished, Melanie lifted him out of his high-chair and put him on the floor because he was a crawling baby. Then Sam wanted to play a game of peek-a-boo with Lily.

And Lily couldn't help laughing because he was so funny.

When Sam was tired, Melanie took him
upstairs for a nap. Then she spread out
some pictures she had cut out of
magazines across the kitchen table.
She fetched some glue and
a big scrapbook.

"Would you like to do
some pasting?" she asked.

"No, thank you," said Lily.

"Well, perhaps you
would like to help
me choose, then,"
said Melanie.

So Lily chose where the different pictures were to go. She chose a piece of cake on a lady's head and a rabbit riding on a fish, a shiny red car in a bed and a building balancing on a chest of drawers. When they had finished, it was a very interesting book.

"You can show it to your dad when he comes to collect you," said Melanie.

Sam was cross when he woke up. He was crying as Melanie carried him downstairs. His nose ran, tears trickled down his cheeks and his mouth was a miserable "O" shape, showing two tiny teeth.

But when he caught sight of Lily, he stopped crying, little by little, and began to hiccup instead.

"He won't do that for me!" said Melanie. "Thank you, Lily."

At lunch time Lily helped to spoon food into Sam's mouth. A lot went into the wrong places but Sam did not seem to mind.

Soon it was time to pick up Sam's big brother,
Jack, from school.

"Don't want to . . ." began Lily.

But Melanie said quickly, "Ringo's coming too and you can help hold his lead if you like."

So Lily held Ringo while Melanie fixed the lead onto his collar.

Lily helped to hold onto Ringo all the way to Jack's school.

Sometimes he pulled on the lead and wanted to run ahead so badly that they could hardly keep up with him.

And sometimes he wanted to stop and sniff around.

They all had to run
the last bit very fast to
get there in time.

Ringo went nearly crazy with joy when Jack came running out of school. Jack had curly hair and a beautiful smile with no front teeth.

When they got back, Jack made some cardboard
boxes into boats and they pretended that Lily and Sam
and Bobbo were sailing far out to sea.

Ringo stayed on the seashore and kept a lookout.

Then they sat together on the sofa and watched television
– all except Sam, who played on the floor. Ringo lay between
Jack and Lily with his head on Lily's lap.

While they were sitting there, Lily heard the doorbell ring.
When Melanie went to answer it, she heard Dad's
voice in the hall.

"You've been having a great time, I hear," he said, putting
his head round the sitting-room door. "I've come to collect
you, as promised."

And he held out Lily's jacket.

But Lily snuggled deeper into the
sofa and hugged Ringo to her chest.
"Don't want to go," she said.

Things to do in February

In the story *Don't Want to Go!*, Lily isn't sure about trying new things. But by the end of the day she's had a lovely time. Here are some new things for you to try in February.

Valentine's Day

Valentine's Day is on 14 February, and it's celebrated in many countries around the world. People celebrate by sending cards, flowers or chocolates to somebody they love.

You can make your own Valentine's card using paper, coloured pens and crayons, glue and glitter: anything you like! Lots of Valentine's cards use the same types of pictures: hearts, flowers, doves and Cupid. Some have rhymes as well. A popular rhyme starts, *"Roses are red, Violets are blue…"* Can you come up with your own ending for the rhyme?

Pancake Day

Pancake Day is usually in February. It's also called Shrove Tuesday and comes before Ash Wednesday, which is the first day of Lent. Lent is the forty-day period before Easter Sunday, and some Christians choose to give something up during this time.

Please ask an adult to help you follow this recipe to make your own pancakes.

Ingredients:
- 100g plain flour, sieved
- small pinch of salt
- 1 large egg
- 300ml semi-skimmed milk
- A little butter

You will need:
- A large bowl
- A fork
- A frying pan

1. Add the salt to the sieved flour in a large bowl.
2. Break the egg into the bowl, and whisk the mixture together with a fork until everything is combined.
3. Now add the milk in small amounts, whisking it in.
4. Ask an adult to cook your pancake for you. They should melt a little butter in a frying pan. When the butter is foaming, pour in enough batter to cover the base of the pan – they should swirl the batter around to coat it evenly. When the underside is gold-coloured, they can flip the pancake or, if they are feeling brave, toss it into the air, then the other side of the pancake can cook through.

Lemon juice and sugar are popular toppings for pancakes, or you can eat them with chocolate spread, jam, golden syrup . . . whatever you like!

Fun with boxes!
Lily has lots of fun playing with a box with Jack. They pretend it's a boat. There are lots of good games you can play with boxes:

- You can get into a big box and pretend it is a boat, a spaceship or a car. What might you want to take into your box with you? Can you decorate the outside of your box?

- Collect shoeboxes, and then glue them together to make a house for your toys. Each box is a room for your dolls, action figures, or toy animals. You can decorate the insides with pictures and by adding furniture. With the help of an adult you can carefully cut out some windows.

Old, empty matchboxes can be drawers, cotton wool balls can be cushions, and bottle tops can be bowls.

- You can make a good indoor den if you have a box big enough to fit inside. You can pretend it's a cave, a house or a castle.

- A box can be a good place to keep special things or to start a collection. Some things you can collect are: shells, stickers, stamps, coins . . .

- Lots of people get coughs and colds in the winter months like Lily's mum in *Don't Want to Go!* You can make a special box for ill days and fill it with interesting things that will help you to feel a bit better.

Scrapbooks
Lily likes helping to carefully cut pictures out of magazines and catalogues and glueing them together. She makes some funny pictures! This is a fun thing to do on a rainy, cold February day. You can make a scrapbook out of the pictures you save from old greetings cards, comics and newspapers.

Daffodil

Sunny, yellow daffodils are a wonderful sign that spring has arrived. Plant bulbs in the autumn and they will brighten up your garden in the spring.

March

March is the month when mad March hares chase each other, leap and tear around. They are wonderful to watch if you are ever lucky enough to see them.

If it's breezy outside you can fly a kite. If it's still wet and chilly you can always make up imaginary indoor journeys, as Alfie and Annie Rose did in my story *A Journey to the North Pole*, or draw maps of exciting explorations. But watch out for crocodiles, bears or other fierce animals!

Lost Sheep

Grandma's house had a long garden at the back and a small garden in front with a gate which led into the lane. If you walked one way you came to the road and more houses. If you walked the other way, up the hill, there were trees, hedges and fields. In the fields lived cows and sheep.

The cows went up to the farm twice a day to be milked. They walked follow-my-leader in a long straggly line. The rest of the time they stayed in the field, munching. Alfie liked the slow way they lowered their necks and pulled up great mouthfuls of grass. When he and Grandma passed by, the cows came to the fence and stood in a row, looking over curiously with big brown eyes, swishing their tails and breathing hard through their noses.

Cows were very nice. But best of all Alfie liked sheep. Sheep were his favourite animals. He especially liked the ones with black faces and bony black legs sticking out below their large woolly bodies.

The field where the sheep lived was further up the hill. When Alfie climbed the gate to say hello to them they trotted away and stood baa-ing at him from a safe distance.

One day, when Alfie and Grandma were out for a walk together, they saw a black-faced sheep standing in the middle of the lane all by herself. She was baa-ing very loudly at the other sheep and they were baa-ing back from behind the fence.

"Oh dear, that sheep's got out somehow," said Grandma.
"She must have got through a hole in the fence."

"I think she wants to get back to the others," said Alfie.

As they came nearer to the sheep, she ran on up the lane. Every so often she stopped and looked through the fence as though she was trying to find a way back. But when Alfie and Grandma came close to try to help her, she shook her woolly tail at them and ran on. She wouldn't let them catch up with her.

The more they hurried behind her, the faster she ran. Soon she had left her own field behind and reached another field full of cows. They put their heads over the fence and moo-ed at her. The poor sheep baa-ed back. She looked very puzzled and lost.

Then she ran on again. She ran to the top of the hill where big trees grew on either side of the lane.

"We'd better not follow her any further," said Grandma. "She'll just run on and on and we'll never be able to catch her."

Alfie and Grandma stood still and wondered what to do.
The sheep stopped too. She stood a good distance away,
but she turned her head to look at them and baa-ed anxiously.

"Let's just stand here for a while and see what happens,"
said Grandma.

Alfie and Grandma stood together hand in hand on the grassy bank. Alfie found it very hard to stand still for long but he pretended he was a tree growing by the fence and that made it easier.

For a long while the sheep just stood and stared at them. Then she started to trot back down the lane towards them. Grandma and Alfie squeezed each other's hands tightly. They stood as still as still. The sheep came nearer and paused. Then she stepped daintily past them, holding up her head proudly and pretending not to notice them at all.

Alfie and Grandma stood and watched her large
woolly back hurrying away round the bend in the lane.
They waited a while before they started to walk home.
When they reached the field where the sheep lived the lane
was empty.

"Our sheep must have found her own way back into
the field with the others," said Grandma.

Alfie climbed the gate to look. The sheep turned
their heads to look back at him. It was very hard to
tell which was the one who had got lost.

"Well done, black-faced sheep!" shouted Alfie,
waving. And all the sheep baa-ed back.

A Journey to the North Pole

Alfie and Annie Rose and Mum were on a visit to Grandma's house. Outside it was cold and wet. Mum was upstairs doing some work on her computer. Alfie and Annie Rose were downstairs in the kitchen with Grandma.

Alfie looked out of the window. It was all steamed up. He could hardly see the garden outside. Raindrops trickled endlessly down the pane. He wrote an "A" for Alfie on it with his finger.

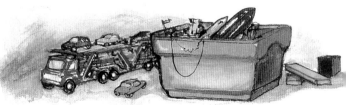

Then he got down on the floor and started to build a Space Station. But Annie Rose kept trying to join in.

"Annie Rose keeps annoying and annoying and annoying me!" wailed Alfie at last. "She won't play with her own toys, she always wants to play with mine!"

"Go away, Annie Rose!" he told her sternly. Then Annie Rose began to cry.

Grandma put down her potato peeler. "Let's go for a walk," she said.

So Alfie and Annie Rose and Grandma struggled into their boots and hats and waterproofs and went out into the rain.

The lane outside
Grandma's gate
had a stream running
down the middle of
it and plenty of mud.
They held hands
and slithered along
together.

It was fun at first, sloshing
about. But soon Annie Rose's
boots were full of water.

Then she sat down in a
puddle and got wet all over.
Alfie's feet were rather damp
too. They turned back towards
home.

"What shall we do now, I wonder?" said Grandma when they were all dry again. "It's not lunchtime yet. I think we had better go on an indoor expedition." Alfie wanted to know what an expedition was and Grandma told him it was a long journey into unexplored territory.

"We'll need supplies," she said. She packed their little backpacks with some crisps and bits of apple and four biscuits, and they set out.

They went through the house pretending that each room they visited was a different country.

They went through jungles, where tigers prowled.

They swam in billowing oceans . . .

and crawled through dense undergrowth . . .

. . . and made boats to cross fast-flowing rivers.

They climbed up steep mountain paths beside rushing waterfalls, hanging on to the rocky sides in case they fell in. And when they reached the top they pitched a tent and ate their supplies.

At last they came to the steep little wooden stairs which led up to Grandma's attic. This was the highest point in the world.

"This is the North Pole all right," said Grandma, shivering. It certainly was cold. They could hear the rain beating down on the roof. But there were so many interesting things there that Alfie and Annie Rose quite forgot they were at the North Pole.

They spent a long time exploring in old suitcases and cardboard cartons full of things which had been dumped down and forgotten.

Annie Rose found some picture postcards and a box with ribbons and bits of jewellery in it, and a handbag and a big hat. Alfie found a broken anglepoise lamp and a set of dominoes and a kite.

"Time to go back to Base Camp," said Grandma.
"Let's take our treasure with us before we freeze to death."
Grandma helped them take it all down to the kitchen.
It was *excellent* treasure. It lasted Alfie and Annie Rose for
the rest of the day until teatime, when the sun came out.

Things to do in March

Become an indoor explorer!
Here are some things you might need to go an an adventure like Alfie and Annie Rose:

- A map. You can either use a real map and pretend, or you can draw a map of the indoor place you're going to explore. Sketch the rooms, doorways and windows, and any large pieces of furniture. Now you need to decide what things are called. Is the North Pole in the attic, like in Alfie's house, or is it at the top of the stairs? Where is the South Pole? Perhaps the bathroom is a watery ocean. Which place is warmest? That could be a sandy desert. If you have a big sofa you can climb onto, that could be Mount Everest!

- Plot your route. What might you need on the way? Will you need to stop off for provisions?

- Now pack your explorer's bag. As well as your map, perhaps you should take a drink, a torch and a compass.

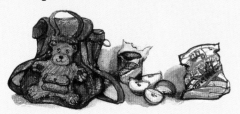

- Dress up in your explorer's outfit: you might need an anorak and a hat, a warm jumper or some sunglasses.

Indoor games
If it's wet outside, it can be fun to learn new indoor games. Do you know how to play Snap? What about Beggar My Neighbour, Go Fish! or Patience? An adult will be able to help you look up the rules to these card games, and after some practice, you can make up your own rules! For instance, some people play a version of Snap with animal noises. At the beginning of the game everyone picks an animal, and instead of saying, *"Snap!"* you must make your animal's noise. To make it harder, you can make the noise of your opponent's animal instead.

Games to play with your hands
There are lots of games you can play with your hands:

Scissors, Paper, Stone
This is a game for two people. You both make a fist with one hand. Then you

count to three, and on three, you both make one of three shapes: Scissors (two fingers out making a cutting motion), Paper (all fingers flat, like a sheet of paper), or Stone (hand in a fist).
In every combination there is a winner and a loser:

- Scissors beat Paper
  (because they cut it).
- Paper beats Stone
  (because it wraps around it).
- Stone beats Scissors
  (because it blunts them).

Thumb Wars
Here, two people clasp each other's hand in a fist, with their thumbs free to move opposite each other. Then they say, *"One, two, three, four, I declare a thumb war."* Each person must try to capture the other's thumb and keep it pressed down for the count of three.

Which Hand?
Choose a small item like a button. Put both your hands behind your back, hold the item in one, then bring your fists to the front. Your opponent must guess which hand the item is in.

Clapping games
There are lots of clapping games and rhymes you can play. One has the song:
Pat-a-cake, pat-a-cake, baker's man,
Bake me a cake as fast as you can.
Pat it and prick it and mark it with T
And put it in the oven for Baby and Me.

You sing this song while clapping your own hands and your partner's in front of you. You can make up your own moves!

Secret handshake
You can make up a secret handshake with someone else – one that only the two of you know. You can use clapping, snapping and wiggling your fingers in any way you like.

Cat's Cradle
Use a long loop of string to make exciting patterns between your hands, twisting and turning it around your fingers. One of the most famous patterns of string is called Cat's Cradle.

You can dance with your hands too. "Doing the Hand Jive" involves patting your thighs, clapping your hands, criss-crossing your hands, bumping your fists together and making thumbs-up signs. Can you make up your own hand-dancing routine?

Primrose

*Primroses are hardy little plants which
can be found in woodland clearings,
hedgerows and gardens. Their flowers
are large and creamy with deeper
yellow centres, and rough textured,
tongue-like leaves.*

April

It's time to get out of doors again, splash through puddles and have a look at what's growing in the garden or the park. This is the month when people get the urge to start digging or planting window boxes. Perhaps you might like to plant something too?

This is the month of Easter, the time of forgiveness and re-birth, of baby birds hatching hopefully out of eggs. And, of course, all those delicious chocolate eggs too.

Alfie's Feet

This little pig went to market,

This little pig stayed
at home,

This little pig had roast beef,

This little pig had none,

And this little pig cried,
Wee-wee-wee-wee-wee,
I can't find my way home.

Alfie had a sister called Annie Rose. Alfie's feet were quite big. Annie Rose's feet were rather small. They were all soft and pink underneath. Alfie knew a game he could play with Annie Rose, counting her toes.

Annie Rose had lots of different ways of getting about. She went forwards, crawling,

and backwards, on her behind,

and she liked to slide
about very fast on her potty,

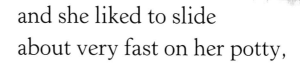

skidding round and round on the floor
and in and out of the table legs.

Annie Rose had
some new red shoes.

She could walk in them a bit, if she
was pushing her little cart or holding
on to someone's hand.

When they went
out, Annie Rose
wore her red shoes
and Alfie wore his
old brown ones.
Mum usually helped
him put them on,
because he wasn't
very good at doing
up the laces yet.

If it had been raining Alfie
liked to go stamping about in
mud and walking through puddles,

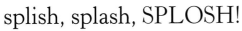
splish, splash, SPLOSH!

Then his shoes got rather wet.

So did his socks,

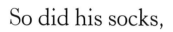

and so did his feet.

So one Saturday morning Alfie and Mum went
to a big shop in the High Street.

They bought a pair of shiny new yellow boots for Alfie to wear when he went stamping about in mud and walking through puddles. Alfie was very pleased. He carried them home himself in a cardboard box.

When they got in, Alfie sat down at once and
unwrapped his new boots. He put them on all
by himself and walked about in them,

stamp! stamp! stamp!

He went into the kitchen to show Mum and Dad
and Annie Rose, stamping his feet all the way,

stamp! stamp! stamp!

The boots were very smart
and shiny but they felt funny.

Alfie wanted to go out again right away. So he put on his mac, and Dad took his book and his newspaper and they went off to the park.

Alfie stamped in a lot of mud and walked through a lot of puddles, splish, splash, SPLOSH! He frightened some sparrows who were having a bath. He even frightened two big ducks. They went hurrying back to their pond, walking with their feet turned in.

Alfie looked down at his feet. They still felt funny. They kept turning outwards. Dad was sitting on a bench. They both looked at Alfie's feet.

Suddenly Alfie knew what was wrong!

Dad lifted Alfie on to the bench beside
him and helped him to take off each boot
and put it on the other foot. And when
Alfie stood down again his feet didn't feel
a bit funny any more.

After tea Mum painted a big black R on to one of Alfie's boots and a big black L on the other to help Alfie remember which boot was which. The R was for Right foot and the L was for Left foot. The black paint wore off in the end and the boots stopped being new and shiny, but Alfie usually did remember to get them on the proper way round after that.

They felt much better
when he went stamping
about in mud and walking
through puddles.

And, of course, Annie
Rose made such a fuss
about Alfie having new
boots that she had to have
a pair of her own to go
stamping about in too,
splish, splash, SPLOSH!

Things to do in April

Puddles

Alfie has lots of fun splashing in puddles – splish, splash, SPLOSH! You can go on your own splashy splashy puddle walk. Make sure you're wearing as much waterproof clothing as possible: warm coat or anorak, hat, gloves, scarf – and, of course, sturdy wellington boots. Then jump in puddles, splash in mud, and come home to get warm and dry!

Looking for rainbows

Rain also means rainbows. Did you know you can make your own rainbow? There are rainbows in the shiny surfaces of CDs, and if you put a bowl of water on a sunny windowsill and shine a mirror at it, you should be able to create a rainbow by angling the reflection onto the wall.

Eggs!

Easter is often in March. Many people give and receive chocolate eggs on Easter Sunday, but eggs can be useful for lots of activities.

Egg rolling

Hold an egg-rolling race. All you need is an egg for each player. Ask an adult to hard-boil and cool your eggs. (If you don't, you will have a messy time when they smash!) You can either find a slope to roll your eggs down, or each player can push their egg along with a wooden spoon. Line up the players and their eggs on the start line, and the first to the finish wins (and the winning egg should be whole and not cracked or broken!).

Egg decorating

You can decorate eggs by painting them or sticking things onto them. Ask an adult to either hard-boil and cool them or blow them. To blow an egg, make a small hole at each end and gently blow the raw egg out of the shell. You could keep the inside to make scrambled eggs or fairy cakes! Now you can paint your eggs, or draw faces on them; glue on stickers, and add wool as hair, fur or a tail. Your egg can be anything you like. *Don't try to eat hard-boiled eggs if they have been out of the fridge for more than two hours.*

The Egg Game

You can also make an egg shape into a face. Eyes, eyebrows and mouths all show how a person is feeling; hats, beards and hairstyles all help. How about wild hair or a green moustache! Will they have big ears or pointy ears?

Baking

Eggs are also important for cooking and baking. This recipe for fairy cakes is for the family to enjoy making together. Children, don't forget that you must have an adult to help you.

Ingredients:
- 125g unsalted butter, softened
- 125g caster sugar
- 1 teaspoon vanilla extract
- 2 large eggs
- 125g self-raising flour, sieved
- 2 tablespoons milk

You will need:
- Baking trays for small fairy cakes
- Paper cases
- A mixing bowl
- A wooden spoon
- Decoration materials!

Makes 12–16 fairy cakes

1. Preheat the oven to 190°C (gas mark 5) and place the paper cases in the baking trays.
2. Cream the butter and sugar together in a bowl. Stir in the vanilla extract.
3. Add the eggs, one at a time, with a spoonful of flour in between. Mix thoroughly.
4. Now add the rest of the flour, again mixing thoroughly.
5. Add the milk and stir it in; if your mixture drops nicely off the spoon, you are ready. If it's still a bit thick, then add more milk.
6. Place a heaped tablespoon of the mixture into each of the paper cases, and ask your adult helper to put them into the oven.
7. Bake for 12 minutes or until cooked through. The cakes should be golden-brown on top, and a skewer inserted into the middle should come out clean.
8. Allow your cakes to cool before decorating them. You can dust with icing sugar or cocoa, or mix some icing sugar with a little water for icing. Decorate your cakes with silver balls, hundreds and thousands, jelly sweets or chocolate buttons – whatever you like!

Did you know . . . ?

People celebrate April Fools' Day on 1 April by playing practical jokes or hoaxes, and then shouting, *"April Fool!"* In Italy, France and Belgium, people stick paper fishes onto each other's back and shout *"April Fish!"* You can only play tricks until midday.

Daisy

Daisies can be found anywhere.
A daisy is actually two flowers in one:
the white outer petals and the cluster of
tiny yellow petals that form the centre.

May

May is the beautiful month when you can play out of doors. It's the month of flowers, of singing and dancing, and making daisy chains.

In May you might take a sketchbook with you when you go out. You could try drawing tiny things, like shells or leaves, or huge things like clouds – but that has to be a quick sketch because they are always changing shape.

The Garden Path

The garden path at Grandma's
Leads past the little pond,
Where nimble golden fishes hide,
To tunnelled leaves beyond.

And through the jungly bit you find
A gate beside a tree,
And a huge world made of grass and sky
As far as you can see.

Looking for Winnie

Alfie's grandma lived in the
country with her two cats, Juno and Belle.
The cats slept in baskets in the kitchen,
near the stove because they liked being
warm. Just up the lane from Grandma's
house lived Jim and Lorna Gatting.
Their son was grown up and had
gone to live far away in New
Zealand. They had a dog called
Shep and a pig and some hens
and two pet tortoises,
Winnie and Fred,
who were very old.
Fred was eighty-
nine and nobody
knew how old
Winnie was; perhaps
nearly a hundred,
Lorna said.

In winter Winnie and Fred were sleepy and liked to be indoors in their cosy boxes full of straw. In summertime they lived outside in the Gattings' back garden. They had a pen with a little wooden house in it and a grassy space with wire around it to stop them getting out. Alfie and Annie Rose often helped to feed Winnie and Fred. They ate bits of lettuce and tomato and they specially liked wild flowers called buttercups.

Alfie often collected a big bunch of them after Jim had cut the grass. He liked watching Winnie and Fred stretch out their leathery necks to nip off the flowers and slowly chew them up in their wide tortoise jaws.

One morning when Alfie and Annie Rose and Grandma went to visit the tortoises, they found Lorna very upset. She told them that when she went out that morning, Fred was there in the pen as usual but Winnie was nowhere to be seen! She was not inside the little house. Lorna had searched in the long grass around the pen but there was no Winnie!

"She must have got out somehow," said Lorna anxiously. "She always was a bit of a wanderer. But she can't have gone far because tortoises are very slow walkers."

Alfie and Grandma and
Annie Rose helped Lorna
to search for Winnie. They
looked all over the garden,
under the bushes and
around the shed.

You can't call or whistle
for a tortoise like you can for
a cat or dog. Anyway, Alfie
had a feeling that Winnie
would not have taken any
notice even if she *had* heard
them calling her.

At supper time Alfie was too worried about Winnie to eat much.

"Perhaps she fell into the pond," he said. "Can Winnie swim?" he asked Grandma.

Grandma was doubtful. "I hope she didn't get into the lane," she said. "I don't like to think of her lying on her back in a ditch. Once tortoises are on their backs they can't get right way up again."

At bed time it was still light and sunny. Grandma said that Alfie and Annie Rose could come with her for one last Winnie hunt.

They set out up the road, looking carefully in the ditch all the way. They walked past the Gattings' house and turned into the lane where old Mrs Hall lived. Still there was no sign of Winnie. Then Grandma said that they really would have to turn back. "Winnie couldn't possibly have got this far anyway," she said.

Mrs Hall's cottage was very neat and tidy, with neat, tidy flowerbeds in her garden. Leading up to the front gate was a neat and tidy path picked out with big round stones on either side, which were painted white.

"Come on, Alfie, it's long past your bed time," said Grandma.

But Alfie hung back. He was looking very hard at Mrs Hall's stones. He noticed that one of them was not white but brown. He ran over to get a closer look, and then he saw that it was not a stone at all, it was Winnie!

"Well spotted, Alfie!" said Grandma, giving him a hug. "I never imagined that Winnie could walk so far. Tortoises can't be such slow walkers after all."

Alfie picked up Winnie and carried her
carefully back to the Gattings' house. Lorna
was delighted. She just could not stop
saying how clever Alfie was to have found
her, and how naughty it was of Winnie to
go off like that and pretend to be a stone.

They carried Winnie into the garden and put her back in the pen. She stretched out her neck and looked about with her beady black tortoise eyes. Alfie and Annie Rose fed her with an extra supply of buttercups.

"I'm *so* glad we've got her back," said Grandma.

But Fred did not seem particularly pleased to see Winnie. He just went inside his shell and would not come out.

Things to do in May

Outdoor games

In May, we're excited to get out into gardens and parks. Here are some fun games to play outside.

Poohsticks

Poohsticks is played on a bridge over a stream or river. Each player chooses a stick and stands on the side of the bridge that is facing upstream (so that the water is flowing towards you, and going under the bridge). On the count of three, everyone drops their stick into the water and then rushes to the other side of the bridge to look for it. The first stick out is the winner; you need to make sure that you pick one you can recognize!

Treasure hunts

In *Looking for Winnie* Alfie and Annie Rose are searching for a lost tortoise. Looking for things can be fun (especially if they are not really lost). Searching for hidden treasure can be an exciting way to pass an afternoon. There are different ways of organizing a treasure hunt:

• Ask an adult to hide a number of items (for instance, marbles or sweets) around a garden or house. Each treasure hunter has a bucket or basket to collect the items in. The winner is the person who finds the most.

• You can also ask an adult to come up with a list of items you need to find – perhaps on a walk in a park or on a beach. Items could include: a white stone, three acorns, a daisy with pink petals . . .

- You can also have a treasure hunt with clues: each clue leads to the next clue, and the last clue leads to the treasure (perhaps some chocolate coins).

Daisy games

Daisies appear in May, and there are some fun things you can do with them. You can ask daisies *"yes"* or *"no"* questions: find the answer by plucking off the petals one by one, saying *"yes"* and then *"no"*, until you arrive at your answer when there are no more petals left.

You can make a daisy chain by picking daisies with long stalks and then making a small slit with your fingernail in the bottom of the stalk. Thread another daisy through this slit, and then join on another daisy, and so on, before joining up your chain and putting it around your neck or head.

Watching things grow

May is a good time to start growing things, either in the garden or on a windowsill. You can grow cress very easily by putting cotton wool into a small container like a clean, empty butter tub. Water the cotton wool and shake some cress seeds onto it. You can arrange the seeds into a shape, if you like. Keep watering the tub so that the cotton wool is always wet. Your cress should be ready to snip and eat in about a week!

You can also grow plants from fruit stones, tops of vegetables or acorns. For example, place old newspaper onto a plate and water it well. Put the top of a carrot onto the plate: in a few days it will have grown roots and you can plant it out in soil, where you will get lovely green growth.

Wild Rose

You'll find roses in gardens or even in woodland. They have lots of petals and a prickly, stiff stem. At the end of summer, roses grow shiny red or orange globes called rose hips.

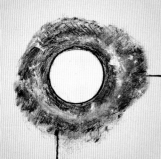

June

June is the magical midsummer month, when fairies are said to come out at night and dance around the fairy ring and the Fairy Queen holds court, as she does in William Shakespeare's famous play *A Midsummer Night's Dream*.

Who knows what may happen when the moon is full? Perhaps even your toys will take off and have secret adventures of their own . . .

Jonadab and Rita

Once there was a girl called
Minnie who lived in a large,
beautiful apartment in Notting
Hill, London. Her mother and
father went off to work each day
very early and did not return
until late at night. Sometimes
they needed to travel abroad.
So Tanya, Minnie's nanny,
looked after her most of the time.

Minnie did not have any pets,
but she had no end of dolls and a
white fluffy monkey and a family
of teddies, all beautifully dressed.
But the most special toy that
Minnie owned (although he did
not know it) was very old and he
was called Jonadab.

Jonadab was a donkey made
of worn grey velvet. His ears
pointed up when he was happy,
and they flopped over when
he was sad. He had belonged
to Minnie's mother and her
grandmother before that.
He had been around in
Minnie's toy box for so long
that these days she did not
take much notice of him.

But Jonadab was not like
other toys. There was one
thing that not even Minnie
or her mother or her
grandmother knew about
him. Which was that
sometimes, very rarely,
when nobody was looking,
Jonadab could fly.

The only other toy who suspected that Jonadab was somehow different from all the others was Rita, a small brown mouse with a multi-coloured tail. But she never told anybody.

When Minnie was very little, she always took Jonadab and Rita in the buggy with her when she and Tanya went walking in Holland Park. Minnie liked chasing the pigeons and making them fly up in front of her with a rush of wings. Jonadab longed to take off after them, but he knew it would never do to show off like that when he was out with Minnie.

These days, sadly, Minnie
hardly ever took Jonadab and Rita
to the park or had them in bed
with her at night. They were such
old friends that she took them for
granted. The white fluffy monkey
was her favourite now.

"It gets very boring being in
the toy box all the time," Jonadab
complained to Rita. "I wish
Minnie would at least talk to us
sometimes."

Rita agreed, but she was
small and used to being easily
overlooked. And when Minnie
did put her on the windowsill with
the other toys, she felt shy and
uncomfortable having to sit next
to the Teddy family who were
always smartly dressed.

Jonadab did not seem to care about his own shabby suit, but he quickly became irritated by the Teddy family's conversation. "They never talk about anything interesting," he remarked crossly. "Unlike you, Rita," he added. And that made Rita feel better.

Rita wondered why Jonadab did not fly away.

"Perhaps I will," he said, "then Minnie would really miss me!"

"I would too," said Rita sadly.

"Oh, I wouldn't be away for long," Jonadab told her.

One night, when a big
midsummer moon was shining
in at the open window, Jonadab
could not bear the stuffy toy box
another minute. Minnie and all the
other toys except Rita were asleep.
Jonadab hopped up onto the toy
cupboard and took a few trial
flights around the room. Then he
poised himself on the windowsill.

"Oh, Jonadab, do be careful,"
squeaked Rita.

"Don't worry, I'll be back,"
Jonadab told her. Then he took
a run across the roof terrace,
launched himself into the blue
night sky and began to fly.

It was a wonderful feeling. He took a couple of turns around the church steeple, then coasted off over the big main street towards Holland Park. Not a single passer-by looked up as he flew overhead.

The park had long been closed for the night, so there was nobody to see him make a perfect landing by the fountain.

"How clever I am," he said to himself. "And how delightful to be out of doors again!"

The park seemed very quiet and magical with no people there. He admired his reflection in the pool.

He strolled around the park until he came to a big grassy space. And this was where he saw the fairies.

At first he thought it was just a trick of the light, but then he saw them plainly. They came crowding down a shaft of moonlight – fairies, elves and gnomes, holding hands and laughing. They surrounded Jonadab at once, stroking his ears and murmuring welcoming things in high sweet voices. They pulled him along to the wild, woody part of the park where no people were allowed to walk, which was where they were having their party.

What a night that was for
Jonadab! The most wonderful
he could ever remember. He
lay on a bed of sweet-smelling
newly mown grass while
the fairies hung garlands of
flowers around his neck and
offered him cups of fairy
wine.

At midnight the Queen
of the Fairies herself arrived,
walking down a moonbeam
followed by her attendants.

She led Jonadab to sit in the place of honour beside her. Then the fairy feast began.

All night long they feasted. Jonadab and the Queen watched as the fairies danced – oh, so lightly – their toes not quite touching the ground.

Just before dawn the Queen and all her elves and fairies began to fade and become transparent. Then, suddenly, they were gone, without saying goodbye, and Jonadab was left alone, with only the twittering birds for company.

"Time to go home," he said to himself. "Minnie will be worrying about me."

The sun was up when he landed on the roof terrace at home. But he found the windows closed. Inside he could see Minnie in her nightdress, singing to her white monkey. He had expected her to welcome him, to kiss and make a great fuss of him. But she had not even noticed he was gone!

Only Rita, who was lying forgotten on the windowsill, saw him. She tried to wave encouragingly to let him know that she at least was glad to see him, but he never looked her way.

Minnie hasn't missed me at all, thought Jonadab sadly. Then he felt very angry. "I'll go back to the park where I am appreciated, so there!" he said, though of course nobody could hear him.

And that is exactly what he did.

He had to wait until dusk before he flew back to the park. He headed straight to the place where he remembered feasting with the fairies the night before and settled down to wait for them to arrive.

He waited and waited. At last a few fairies arrived, strolling down a moonbeam with their arms around each other's waists. Jonadab galloped happily towards them. But tonight everything seemed different. The fairies did not seem to recognize him.

"It's me, Jonadab!" he greeted them. But the fairies looked at him blankly, as though he were a complete stranger, then walked on, whispering among themselves.

Jonadab trailed after them, but it was no use. How was he to know that fairies were famous for their short memories and even shorter friendships? They had simply forgotten him.

"When is the Queen due to arrive?"
Jonadab asked one of them.

She turned round and said, "Oh, didn't
you know? The Queen isn't coming
tonight. She's holding a grand reception
on the other side of the moon."

Jonadab watched the fairies disappear
into the wild place where they had danced
the night before. For a while he glimpsed
them flitting among the tree trunks. Then
they seemed to fade and disappear.

Suddenly he felt terribly alone. I can't
go back now, he thought. Minnie has
forgotten me and now the fairies don't
want me either. And if the park keepers
find me, they'll put me into Lost Property
and what will become of me then?

He huddled down miserably under a
bench, dreading the morning.

Back at the apartment, Minnie was up early as usual arranging her dolls when she caught sight of Rita, still tangled up in the curtain. And it was at that moment that she suddenly thought of Jonadab.

She remembered that she had hardly played with him for a long time. She started looking for him in the toy boxes and cupboards and all over the room, but he was nowhere to be found. And all at once Minnie did not want her teddies or her dolls or her white monkey. Tears started in her eyes. "Oh, Rita," she said, "wherever has he got to?"

Minnie was too upset to eat her lunch. When it was time for her and Tanya to go to the park, she took Rita for company, tucked into her pocket with only her ears and eyes poking out. All along the leafy walks, where Minnie usually ran joyfully, she now trailed behind, walking more and more slowly. At last she stopped altogether.

"Come along, Minnie!" called Tanya, far ahead. It was then that Rita spotted a sad, bedraggled shape slumped under a bench – Jonadab!

But now Minnie was following Tanya. Soon they would have left Jonadab behind. Rita did not know what to do. She could not speak human language. She could not move. She was too frightened even to give a reassuring squeak to Jonadab to show that she had seen him.

Then an extraordinary thing happened. It was a kind of magic. Somehow (she never knew how) Rita managed to screw herself up and launch herself right out of Minnie's pocket. She somersaulted through the air and landed on the path just near where Jonadab was hiding.

She lay there, exhausted by the effort. "I never knew I could fly," she whispered breathlessly to herself. "I've never done it before and I don't suppose I'll ever be able to do it again. But what now? Has Jonadab seen me? Has Minnie noticed I've gone? Oh, Jonadab! Oh, Minnie! Oh, help!"

Then something worse happened. A lady came round the corner with a great bounding dog. When he saw Rita lying there, he stopped and sniffed her. Then he licked her and pushed her about with his nose.

When the dog picked her up in his jaws, Rita thought: This is the end of me! My last moment has come!

"Put that down, Sandy!" cried the dog's owner. The dog dropped Rita and began to bark.

At that moment Minnie stopped still. She had heard the barking. She turned round. Now she was feeling in her pocket. She had realized Rita was gone!

And now she was running back as fast as she could to rescue her!

When Minnie bent to pick her up, Rita longed to cry out, "Please, please, Minnie, look under the bench!"

But the dog was already doing
just that. He was sniffing around.
He had found a new toy. He
picked up Jonadab in his jaws and
shook him this way and that. Then
he ran over to his owner and laid
him at her feet.

"What dirty old thing have
you found now?" said the lady.
But Minnie shrieked out:
"That's not a dirty old thing!
That's my Jonadab!"

A great commotion followed.
Tanya ran up, the dog barked
and leaped about while the lady
pulled his collar.

But Minnie, in the midst of it
all, was clutching Jonadab very
tightly with one hand and Rita
with the other as though she
would never again let them go.

When at last they were safely home again, Minnie laid Rita and Jonadab tenderly in her own bed. "Oh, Jonadab! However did you get so far from home?" she asked. But Jonadab said nothing. After Minnie had sung them a little song and thought they were asleep she whispered: "Dear Jonadab, dear Rita, how terrible it would have been if I had lost you."

Much later, when Minnie herself was fast asleep beside them, Jonadab told Rita all about his adventures.

"A fairy feast!" squeaked Rita. "How I would love to have seen it!"

"Yes, it was remarkable of course," said Jonadab. "And the Queen is very beautiful. But I don't plan to do any more flying for the moment. I think I'll stay at home for a bit now."

"Won't it seem a bit dull?" Rita asked him.

"Oh, no, I think not," said Jonadab. "You see, the fairies haven't the gift of true friendship as you have, Rita. It was you who saved me. You will always be a true heroine."

And Rita gave a big, happy sigh.

Things to do in June

Midsummer

On 21 June we celebrate Midsummer's Day – the longest day of the year. In *Jonadab and Rita* Jonadab experiences a magical midsummer, meeting fairies and taking flight. Summer is a great time for daydreaming and telling stories. You can read stories from books (visit your local library to find new stories) or make up your own. Telling stories on a picnic rug outside can be lots of fun, and you can play storytelling games too. For instance, one person starts telling a story, and at an exciting point hands over to the next person, who must continue it.

Midsummer games

In summer you can fly kites or learn to juggle – first with two balls and then with three. Or play Piggy in the Middle, in which two people throw a ball to each other and a third (the Piggy) stands in between and tries to intercept it. If the Piggy is successful, then he or she swaps places with whoever threw the ball – who becomes the new Piggy.

Races

For some races it's good to be fast; for some, you need to have a steady hand, be gymnastic or skilful in different ways – for example, throwing an object as far as you can (take care not to break or lose anything!). You can hold a special event: try out different types of race, and make medals from decorated cardboard to give to the winners.

Here are some other ideas:

Egg-and-spoon race

For this you need a hard-boiled egg for each person (or you can use a ball), and a spoon which the egg or ball will fit into. The players race over the course, without letting the egg fall off the spoon.

Balloon race

Each player needs a balloon, and must bat it in the air from the start to the finish line.

Three-legged race

For this race you must compete in pairs. Each pair ties their ankles together with a scarf or belt and races to the finish. Coordination is the key!

Wheelbarrow race

You need to be in pairs for this race too. One person is the wheelbarrow, with their hands on the ground while the other person holds their legs.

Stepping stones

Each player needs two sheets of newspaper. You must follow the course, stepping only on your sheets of newspaper: you must pick up and put down each sheet of paper as you move forwards.

Obstacle race

Create a course in which you need to get past different obstacles – for example, jumping over a skipping rope, avoiding the cracks in paving stones, or crawling under a chair.

Look closer

In summer, it's good to experience things outside: you can look for different flowers, leaves and trees, and listen out for the songs of different birds. It can also be fun to look closely at a tiny patch of ground and count all the different things you can see. Pick a patch and study it for ten minutes, counting all the insects, types of plants and objects you spot.

Dandelion

You can "tell the time" with dandelions
by blowing the delicate seeds from the
stem – the number of blows it takes to clear
all the seeds is thought to tell the time of day.

July

July is the month for summer adventures, like camping, exploring, going on picnics and making outdoor dens. You can even make one in your own back garden.

In July, when the grass is high, and you climb to the top of a hill, who knows what you may see on the other side?

And on a clear night, when the sky is full of stars, you can pick out the amazing patterns they make, far, far away from us on earth.

Where's Alfie?

Where's Alfie?
Nobody knows.
Annie Rose is calling him.
She wants him to play with her.
But there's no answer.
Because Alfie's in his secret den
At the bottom of the garden.
He's in there among the leaves
Where nobody can see him.
Not answering when he is called.
Flumbo is in there with him.
They've got provisions: a sandwich,
    a bottle of orange juice and three biscuits.
That should last for a bit.
They're planning to be a secret gang one day,
    like Robin Hood and his outlaws living in the forest.
But in the meantime, Alfie's got some special things
    in there, which nobody knows about.
There's an old key that he found in the ground,
And a precious piece of china with a blue and white pattern on it,
And a little plastic teddy.
Alfie keeps them under some leaves, where nobody can find them.
Because this is his special place.
It's his secret den.
He could even stay out here all night if he felt like it.
Well, until bedtime anyway.

Alfie Upstream

One hot summer afternoon,
when Alfie and Annie Rose
and Mum and Dad were
staying with Grandma,
Mum and Alfie decided to
go exploring. It was going
to be just the two of them.
Annie Rose was going to
stay behind in the garden
with Dad. They set out
through the little gate into
the field. Jim Gatting's pig
was lying flat on its stomach
under the big tree. It was
too hot to take any notice
of them.

They walked right across
the field until it began to
slope steeply down to where
trees and thick bushes grew.
Alfie had never been this
far before.

It was then that they heard the sound of running water. Alfie was very excited. They climbed under some wire and there, in the thick green shade, they found a little running stream.

"Now we're real explorers," said Mum.

The stream was shallow and had a gravelly bottom and floating weeds. Alfie and Mum took off their shoes and waded in. It was beautifully cool.

They splashed along.
It was very quiet except
for the buzzing insects
and the sound the water
made. Sometimes
they came to some
squelchy muddy bits
and sometimes a big
stone in the middle
of the stream which
they had to climb
over. And once Alfie
saw a dragonfly with
shimmering wings
hovering over the
surface.

Then they came to
a place where a tree
had fallen down, like a
bridge across the water.

Beyond that the stream widened into a little pool.
It was deeper there. It came up to above Alfie's knees,
but he and Mum were brave explorers and didn't care
about a little thing like wet shorts.

They climbed on to the bank. There was a smooth grassy space, and in the middle of it a little apple tree with branches which hung over the stream. The apples were still hard and green. They sat with their feet in the water and threw little apples in to see which would make the biggest plop.

Mum stretched out on the grass. "I think
we've found the Garden of Eden, Alfie,"
she said sleepily. Right away Alfie wanted
to know what kind of a garden that was.

So Mum told Alfie the story of how, at the beginning of the world when all the plants and fishes and birds and animals were brand new, there were only two people on earth: a man and a woman called Adam and Eve. And they lived in a beautiful garden called Eden and were free like the animals.

A river ran through the garden and they had all they needed to eat. But there was one fruit they were not allowed to pick, and that was an apple from a very special tree.

But one day the snake, who was full of cunning, told Eve to pick the apple.

Eve knew she shouldn't but she just couldn't resist it.

So she took a bite and so did Adam. And after that things were never the same again.

Adam and Eve had to leave the Garden of Eden for ever. They could never go back because the gate was guarded by an angel with a flaming sword. And from that day on they were no longer free like the animals. They had to work hard for their living.

"Like Dad and me," said Mum.

Alfie thought about this. "Well, I hope the apple was a nice juicy one, anyway, not all hard and green like these ones are."

Just at that moment a very surprising thing happened.

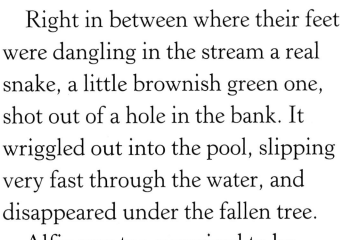

Right in between where their feet were dangling in the stream a real snake, a little brownish green one, shot out of a hole in the bank. It wriggled out into the pool, slipping very fast through the water, and disappeared under the fallen tree.

Alfie was too surprised to be frightened. "Just like the story," he whispered.

Mum said, "It wouldn't have hurt us. It was too busy minding its own business."

They sat there without talking for quite a long while until it was time to go home. And neither Alfie nor Mum ever forgot that time and that place.

Things to do in July

Making dens

In *Alfie Upstream* Alfie goes on an adventure with his mum: they find an exciting new place, and he hears a new story. And in *Where's Alfie?* we find Alfie in his secret den. It's exciting to make an outside den in summer. You can use boxes (just like an indoor den) or get help to put up a tent, or drape sheets over washing lines or chairs. In your den, you can have a picnic, play card games, draw, or play with toys, or you can tell stories like Alfie and his mum.

Secret codes

If you make a secret den, then you might like to create a secret club, and use special invisible ink to write secret messages. Lemon juice, orange juice, apple juice and milk all work well as invisible ink. Put some in a bowl, and use your finger or a thin, blunt stick to dip into the "ink" and write on the paper. It will look invisible, but the message will appear if you heat up the paper next to a radiator or out in the sun. Or you can make up your own code – write out the letters of the alphabet, and then jumble them up, making a note of which letters become which: an A may become an E, and so on.

Bubbles!

Do you know how to blow bubbles? Ask an adult to help you mix one part washing-up liquid with six parts water, and then dip a bubble wand or straw into it and blow! Who can blow the biggest bubble? There are rainbows in the bubbles – can you catch one?

Car games

Some people head off on holiday at this time of year. Here are some games that you can play in the car:

I Spy

Pick something you can see out of the window (for example, a post box). Then say, "I spy, with my little eye, something beginning with P." The other people in the car have to guess what you have spotted.

Cows and Sheep

For this game, half the people in the car are Cows, and half are Sheep. The Cows get one point for every cow they see, and the Sheep get one point for every sheep. You can make up other rules too: for example, you get five points for a horse, or lose points if you see a tractor.

The Alphabet Game

Take it in turns to find things beginning with each letter of the alphabet: the first person spots something beginning with A, the second something beginning with B, and so on.

The Sentence Game

Each person in turn says one word to make up a funny sentence or story. For example: *Bob Loves Cold Spaghetti And His Nose Is Green.*

The Number Plate Game

Pick a number plate and look at the letters in it – can you make a word from them? A number plate with a B, an A and an L in it might be BALL, or BALLET or BAUBLE!

Animal impressions

Take it in turns to do impressions of animals: the other players have to guess what animal you are.

Sunflower

*Just sow sunflower seeds in a
sunny, sheltered spot and watch them
grow and grow! During the day
sunflowers tilt to face the sun and
slowly follow it around in the sky.*

August

This is the time for holidays, for
packing up your bucket and spade and
heading for the seaside. There are endless
games you can play on the beach. But
best of all is to dig a sandcastle with a moat,
watch the tide come in and surround it,
then wash over it until there is nothing left.

At low tide there are rockpools to
explore – whole worlds where all kinds
of creatures live among the seaweed
and mud.

Summer Numbers

Ten tall aerials, pointing at the sky,
Nine brown birds, swooping by,
Eight parked cars, baking in the street,
Seven pretty flower pots, lined up neat,
Six hot schoolboys, trailing home late,
Five friendly neighbours, chatting by the gate,
Four lazy cats, sitting in the shade,
Three laughing ladies, sipping lemonade,
Two squealing children, playing with the hose,
One of them is Alfie and the other's –
Annie Rose!

Alfie Goes Camping

One summer afternoon Mum hung a sheet over the washing line and weighted it down with stones on either side. Alfie crawled inside. It made a good tent.

"I'm camping," Alfie called out. "This is my tent and nobody can come in here unless I say so!"

But Annie Rose was already coming in through the other end, uninvited.

Alfie went indoors and brought out some important things to put in his tent. He brought a colouring book and some crayons, a saucepan, his old blanket and his knitted elephant. He spread a rug inside and some cushions to sit on.

"Real campers cook their food over a camp-fire and eat it sitting on the ground," Alfie told Annie Rose. So they put some bits of grass into the saucepan and cooked them over a pretend fire.

After that they went inside the tent and lay down on the cushions. Alfie pretended it was night-time and there was a forest all around full of wolves, snakes and snarling tigers.

Annie Rose was not quite sure whether she liked this part of the game, and she soon trotted indoors to find Mum.

Alfie was still in his tent when Dad came home from work. He brought out a mug of tea and drank it sitting by Alfie's camp-fire.

Dad told Alfie that he had owned a real tent when he was a boy and had slept out in it all night.

"I'll look in the loft and see if it's still there," he promised. "And if it is, we might try it out next time we go to visit Grandma in the country."

Dad did find the tent. Alfie was very excited when the
time came to put it up in the field next to Grandma's house.
Everyone came out to watch. It was big enough for two people
to lie down in.

Annie Rose was too little to go camping so it was going to be just Alfie and Dad. They had brought proper foam mattresses and sleeping bags with them from home.

"I hope it doesn't rain," said Dad.

Alfie could hardly wait until bedtime. He kept going in and out of the tent to check that everything was  ready. He had put his blanket and elephant beside his sleeping bag. Dad had put an electric torch beside his.

 At last bedtime came. Alfie had a wash and put on his pyjamas and dressing gown just as usual. He wanted to cook his own supper over a camp-fire but Dad said that might be a bit difficult.

Instead they had supper in the kitchen, jacket potatoes and baked beans. Grandma gave them some apples to take with them into the tent.

Then they set out. It was strange not to be going upstairs to bed but down the garden, through the gate and into the field.

It was still light. Dad and Alfie sat down in front of the tent with a blanket around them and ate their apples. They watched the sun go down behind the trees. They watched the sky change colour. They saw the birds swooping and calling to one another. They sat there until it was quite dark and the stars came out, one by one.

It was very mysterious to be outside at night under the big sky, with rustling noises all around and the wind blowing the branches about. But Alfie felt very safe being there with Dad.

Just before it was time to settle down, Alfie jumped up, scampered off across the field, and did a little dance all by himself under the stars.

Then they climbed into their sleeping bags and Alfie cuddled up to his blanket with his elephant beside him and went off to sleep.

When he woke up it wasn't morning. It was the middle of the night. It was completely dark, not like being in a bedroom with the light shining in from the landing, but pitch-black all around.

Alfie put out his hand. He could feel Dad's back next to him, humped up inside the sleeping bag. Alfie lay very still and listened. He could hear noises outside, strange creakings and flappings.

Inside the tent he could hear Dad breathing. But then Alfie realized that he could hear something else breathing too. And that something was *outside the tent*!

Alfie sat up. He didn't scream. He didn't even cry. He just leaned over and wrapped his arms around Dad's neck and squeezed very tightly indeed. Then, of course, Dad woke up too.

Now the breathing thing was just near their heads. It was a very snorty, snuffly sort of breathing. They could hear it moving, too. It was trampling about in the grass. Then it went round the tent to the zip opening, which Dad had left not quite done up, and started to push against it.

Alfie was quite sure that something huge and horrible was coming to eat them up. He began to scream and scream.

"It's OK, Alfie," said Dad. He felt for his torch and switched it on.

They saw a big pink nose coming through the tent flap.
It had very large wet nostrils.

"It's a pig!" said Dad. And he bravely got out of his sleeping
bag and gave the nose a big push.

Alfie stopped screaming. He and Dad crawled out of the
tent. It did not seem quite so dark outside. The pig moved a
short distance away and stood there watching them.

"I didn't know Jim Gatting had put his pig in this field," grumbled Dad sleepily. He tried to make the pig go away but it wouldn't.

After a while they tried to go back to sleep in the tent but the pig kept trying to join them.

In the end there was nothing for it but to take the tent down. They collected up all their things and carried them back into Grandma's garden. It took several journeys to and fro. The pig followed closely behind them.

When Dad finally closed the garden gate on the pig, it stuck its snout through the bars and watched them.

Dad told Alfie that they couldn't very well wake up everybody in the house at that time of night, so they had better put up the tent again in the garden. Alfie thought that was a very good idea.

At last they got the tent back up and crawled into it, and the pig got tired of watching and wandered off down the field.

Alfie and Dad dozed until it was nearly light.

When Alfie woke again, Dad was still fast asleep. Alfie crept quietly out of his sleeping bag and stood in the wet grass in his bare feet. The curtains of Grandma's house were still tightly drawn. But the sun was up and the birds were making a great noise.

Alfie felt very special to be the only person awake and out of doors that sunny morning. And he made up his mind to ask Dad if they could go camping again that very night.

Things to do in August

In *Alfie Goes Camping* Alfie sleeps outside in a tent. The sky is very beautiful on a clear summer's night. Ask an adult if you can stargaze together. Can you see the Plough, or Orion's Belt?

Shadow puppets

If you are staying in a tent, you can use the wall of the tent and a torch to make shadow animals. Use your hands to make shadows – of birds, rabbits and other animals. Other people can try to guess what creature you are making.

Fun on the beach

There are lots of things to do on the beach in summer.

Rock-pooling

Rock pools are fascinating to look into: you can find seaweed, and creatures clinging to the rocks, like barnacles and mussels. You might be lucky and see a fish, a crab, a starfish or a sea urchin.

Beachcombing

You can collect things on the beach too: beautiful shells, unusual stones, and pieces of flotsam and jetsam. Get a bucket and start looking for hidden treasure. Who can gather the most interesting things? Once you get home, glue small shells onto a box to keep your beachcomber treasures in.

Sandcastles

Who can make the biggest and best sandcastle? You can use shells and seaweed to decorate it, dig a moat, and even stand inside if it's big enough!

Sand angels

You can make sand angels by lying on your back in the sand and moving your arms and legs up and down across it. When you get up it will look like you have wings.

Hand Cricket

For this game you need only a ball and your hand. One person is the bowler, another the batsman, while the others are fielders.

Duck, Duck, Goose

In this game, all the players sit in a circle, except for one, who walks around them, touching each person's head and saying *"Duck"*. At a certain point, he or she suddenly says *"Goose!"* and runs round the circle; the "Goose" has to jump up and run round in the opposite direction. Whoever gets back to the space first sits down; the one left standing begins to walk around the circle, and the game starts again.

Bonting

One fine morning Alfie went into his back garden and found a very special stone. He put it in his pocket and he called it Bonting. Many children have their own special Bonting – an interesting stone. Some have whole collections, beautifully painted. You can find lovely Bontings everywhere. If you don't have a garden, the park or the seaside are excellent places to look for them.

Poppy

*Poppies have four large red petals
which drop off at the merest touch.
They are a common "weed" amongst
crops, sometimes making entire fields
look red from a distance. Poppies are
used as a symbol to remind people
of soldiers who have died in war.*

September

September is just as much a time of promise and new beginnings as the spring; time to start the new school year, to make new friends and catch up with old ones. Eid-al-Fitr – the end of Ramadan – is often celebrated in September, when family and friends gather and give thanks.

It's still warm enough to play outside and try out some new skipping or ball games in the playground. In the countryside there's fruit-picking and blackberrying. What is more delicious than apple crumble or bramble jelly?

Bobbo Goes to School

It was Monday morning and Mum was loading the washing machine. Lily wasn't helping. She was hiding Bobbo amongst the towels and sheets.

"Oh, do stop that, Lily," said Mum, "or I'll never get this done."

Lily stopped. But then she started to throw Bobbo into the air and catch him by the leg. Bobbo could tell it was going to be one of Lily's bad days.

After Mum had turned on the washing machine it was time to go shopping. She pulled Lily's sweater over her head and pushed her arms into the sleeves. Lily did not help. She went all limp like a rag doll.

"Shall we take Bobbo?" said Mum. "I'm sure he'd like to come."

Lily stopped going limp, and together they looked for Bobbo. They found him hiding under a cushion. At last they were ready to set off.

While Lily and Bobbo were waiting on the pavement for
Mum to open up the buggy, they saw the school bus draw up.

The driver got out and helped the school children to jump on board. Then he got in again and started the engine.

Just as the bus was pulling away,
Lily did a dreadful thing. She swung
Bobbo round and round by his leg and
threw him high into the air – just like
that! Bobbo flew up head first and
landed smack on the roof of the bus,
just as it was pulling out into the traffic.

Lily and Mum were too shocked to move.
They both stood there and watched as the
bus gained speed and disappeared.

"Bobbo! I want him back!" wailed Lily.
But it was too late. Bobbo was gone.

Lily and Mum rushed back indoors
and Mum got on the phone straight away.
She spoke to the lady at the school and
told her that Bobbo would soon be
arriving on top of the school bus
and would they please rescue him.

Lily cried and cried.
"He might fall off and
get run over!" she
howled. "And I won't
see him again ever!"

In fact Bobbo had not fallen off. He was lying face up, rushing along very fast and looking up at the sky. Sometimes he slipped a bit, but he stayed on board. This was all rather exciting for Bobbo. He had never travelled on a bus without Lily before.

Down below the children laughed and chatted and looked out of the bus window. They would never have imagined that Bobbo was riding on the roof of their bus.

Soon they arrived at the school. The driver pulled up near the entrance doors, and that sent Bobbo straight into a bush.

It felt like being a bird. For a moment he thought he *was* a bird. He felt rather tired after all this excitement, so he just lay there, swaying gently and wondering what would happen next.

What an extraordinary day this was turning out to be for Bobbo!

Back at home Lily's day was going from bad to worse. Mum telephoned the school again.

But the lady who answered said that the driver had looked on top of the bus and no soft toy had been found there.

Lily wept. It was terrible to think that she had thrown away her oldest, dearest friend.

"I want Bobbo back *now*!" she sobbed.

Meanwhile, as
Bobbo was resting
among the leaves,
the school children
came out to play.

A little girl called Natasha, who was playing under the bush with her friend, found Bobbo and handed him to the teacher.

All the children crowded round and made a great fuss of him. No one knew where he had come from.

So they took him to their classroom and put him in a special place on the Interest Shelf where he could see everything.

He sat there for the rest of the morning while the children did counting and drew pictures and listened to a story.

When the lady in the school office heard that Bobbo had been found, she telephoned Mum and Lily and they drove to the school straight away. Lily was allowed to go into the classroom to collect him. When she saw him on the Interest Shelf, she ran straight over and hugged him tightly.

Then the teacher and children showed
Lily what they had been doing with Bobbo.

They told her that they had been playing a game: they were trying to guess what his name was. Each of them had written their guess down.

Lily told them that none of them had got it right because his name was Bobbo!

She was very happy when she thanked them and said goodbye.

"Oh, what a relief that we've found him!" said Mum when at last they arrived back home. "I think he liked it at school, and you'll like it too, Lily, when you're old enough to go there."

Lily was hugging Bobbo very tightly, pressing her face against his nose. "I'll never, never throw you away again!" she whispered.

Bobbo said nothing.
Lily's bad day had turned
out well after all.

Things to do in September

Playground games

This is back-to-school time and there are lots of playground or park games you can play: ball games, skipping games, and running games.

Hopscotch

Do you know how to play Hopscotch? You need to mark out a hopscotch grid outside – you can use paving slabs and draw the numbers 1 to 10 on them. When you are ready to play, throw a stone onto the hopscotch grid – you then have to hop up the grid from 1 to 10, missing out the number that the stone has landed on, and then hop back, picking up the stone on the way.

Skipping games

Skipping games have lots of different rhymes and moves. You can skip on your own with an ordinary rope:

practise skipping on one foot, or even backwards! If you have a longer rope, you can skip with a group of friends: two people can hold the ends, while the one in the middle skips, before you swap over. If you get really good, you can try it with two ropes, and with more than one person skipping.
Here's a popular skipping rhyme:

Teddy Bear, Teddy Bear, turn around,
Teddy Bear, Teddy Bear, touch the ground,
Teddy Bear, Teddy Bear, show your shoe,
Teddy Bear, Teddy Bear, that will do!
Teddy Bear, Teddy Bear, go upstairs,
Teddy Bear, Teddy Bear, say your prayers,
Teddy Bear, Teddy Bear, turn out the lights,
Teddy Bear, Teddy Bear, say good night!

The person skipping must try and perform the actions mentioned in the song.

Indoor games

As the weather gets colder, it's good to think of indoor games to play. Here are some pen and paper games:

Paper dolls

All you need is a long strip of paper, which you fold into a concertina, leaving a top piece which is big enough to draw your first doll onto. The arms should reach to the very edges of the paper so that your paper dolls will all be holding hands. Ask an adult to help you cut round your doll through all the folded pieces of paper. When you extend the paper like a concertina, there will be lots of dolls, holding hands, ready for you to decorate.

Heads, Bodies and Legs
This drawing game can be played with as many people as you like – or just two. Each player needs a piece of paper and a pencil, and starts by drawing a head at the top of the paper. How many eyes and ears and noses and mouths does it have? Now you fold the paper down so that the drawing can't be seen any more. However, it's useful if the next person can see the bottom of the neck so that they can join the body to it. Swap your papers and draw a body on the next piece of paper – let your imagination run wild! Fold the paper down again, leaving the very bottom of the body showing so that the legs can be joined on at the next stage. Swap papers and draw your legs! Fold down a final time, swap and have a look at your creations! Can you come up with a name for your creature?

Things to spot and find
September is the perfect time to go blackberrying. You will need something to hold your blackberries, like a basket, jam jar or plastic container. Make sure you dress in clothes that protect you from prickles. Go blackberrying with an adult who can pick the high-up ones, and make sure you wash them.

There are acorns all over the ground in autumn. You can grow an acorn in a clear container, like a bottle with a narrow neck. Fill the bottle up with water, then place the acorn in the neck. Soon you will see roots growing, and a green shoot. You will need to keep the water topped up.

Have you seen sycamore seeds falling from the trees? They look like helicopters as they twirl round and round on their way to the ground.

Michaelmas Daisy

*If Michaelmas daisies are picked
and kept in a vase they can last more
than a fortnight! They can be found
in a wide range of colours, including
deep pinks, plums and purples.*

October

October is Harvest Festival time, when gardeners proudly show off their best home-grown vegetables. This is the season when there are conkers to collect, and the leaves turn to all sorts of wonderful colours before they fall. Have you ever tried collecting different-shaped leaves? Perhaps you could draw and colour them.

This is the month of Halloween, of lighted pumpkins, when there may be witches about, flying through the air on their broomsticks!

Alfie Wins a Prize

One Saturday morning when Alfie and Annie Rose had finished their breakfast, Dad said he was thinking of taking them to the Harvest Fair at the Big School that afternoon. Alfie and Annie Rose liked fairs, where there were usually interesting things to look at and good things to eat.

"There's going to be a pet show and a children's painting competition too," Dad told Alfie.

Alfie wanted to take their cat Chessie along and put her into the pet show. He was sure she would win a prize. But Mum said that Chessie wasn't the sort of cat who would like being in a show, and that it might put her into a cross mood.

"What about painting a picture instead?" Dad suggested.

Alfie thought that was a good idea. He liked painting. Mum found a piece of paper and a paint brush and they cleared a space on the table. Then they got out the paints that Grandma had given them and Mum showed Alfie how to wash out his brush so the colours would not get mixed up and turn muddy.

"What shall I paint?" Alfie asked.

Mum thought. Then she fetched the jug, which had yellow and orange leaves, red berries and mauve daisy flowers in it, and put it on the table. "These are pretty, don't you think?" she said.

But Alfie did not want to paint leaves and berries. He already had a better idea. He dipped his brush carefully into the paint and began his picture.

When he had finished everyone was very interested to see what he had painted. "I like all that red and black," said Dad. "It's a face, I can see that. Is it some sort of bird?"

"No," said Alfie, "it's a motorbike man. These are his eyes and this is his red helmet. And these are his black gloves."

Mum helped Alfie to write his name under his picture. Then she wrote at the top: "Children's Painting Competition – 5 and Under: MOTORBIKE MAN". And she stuck the picture up on the door of the fridge so that they could all admire it while they had lunch. Then they set out for the Harvest Fair. Alfie carried his painting, carefully rolled.

The first people they saw in the Big School hall
were Maureen MacNally and her mum. They had
made an enormous cake and were inviting people
to guess how much it weighed. The person who
guessed nearest was going to win the cake.

Then Alfie and Mum and Dad and Annie Rose went
to look at all the flowers and fruit and vegetables,

and second-hand toys,

and home-made cakes and fudge.

Then they went into the school playground
to look at the pet show.

Min and her little sister Lily had brought their beautiful rabbits. They let Alfie and Annie Rose stroke them. The white rabbit, Bianca, had pink eyes. Domino's eyes were like shiny dark brown beads.

Bernard had put his pet beetle into the show. It lived in a jam jar amongst a lot of leaves.

"You can't see him because he's hiding," Bernard told Alfie. "He may come out later if he feels like it."

Bernard was going in for the children's painting competition too, so they all went off together. When they got there Bernard unrolled his picture and held it up for Alfie and Annie Rose to see. "It's two slime monsters having a fight," he told them.

Bernard was not a careful painter. There was a lot of slime and red blood dripping all over the picture. But Alfie and Annie Rose thought it was very good.

A lot of other children were handing in their pictures and a teacher was pinning them up on big screens.

Alfie's "Motorbike Man" was pinned up with the other pictures. Everyone was gathering round to look.

Some children had done cars, trucks and spaceships. The Santos twins had both painted bugs and butterflies.

Kevin Turley had done a picture of his mum. Louise Harper had painted a blue house with a lot of smoke coming out of the chimney, and Rahima Shariff had done a beautiful picture of orange and yellow leaves and berries and a big red apple.

On a table nearby were the prizes. The first prize for the 5 and Unders was a picture book about dinosaurs. The second prize was a jigsaw puzzle of a farmyard scene and the third prize was a bottle of bright green bubble bath.

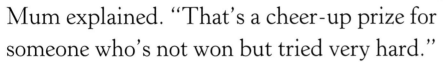

Behind them sat a sad, stuffed, woolly animal. Alfie was not sure whether he was a sheep or a goat.

"He's a consolation prize," Mum explained. "That's a cheer-up prize for someone who's not won but tried very hard."

The consolation prize's ears were lopsided, and he wore a jersey with orange buttons. Alfie stared at him but he didn't look back. He had his nose in the air, as if he were trying not to mind about not being a proper prize like the others.

Everyone waited around while the judges looked at the pictures.

But now at last the winners were being announced!

First prize – Rahima Shariff!

Second prize – Kevin Turley!

Third prize . . .

. . . Alfie!

Everyone clapped and cheered. Alfie stepped up all by himself and shook hands with the lady who was presenting the prizes. She gave him the green bubble bath and told him that she thought his picture was "colourful and original". Last of all it was announced that the consolation prize went to Louise for her blue house. It was all very exciting. Alfie's friends crowded around him. All except Bernard, that is.

He was very upset that his painting of slime monsters had not won. He told Alfie that he thought all the prizes were silly.

Louise was not at all happy either.

"She's rather down in the dumps, I'm afraid," her dad told Alfie's dad later when they were having tea together. "She had set her heart on the green bubble bath."

"Soft toys are babyish," said Louise.

And she shoved the consolation prize down on the floor
beside her chair. He sat there with his nose still proudly in
the air. Of course, Alfie knew that toys cannot understand
anything. But secretly he hoped that the sheep (or goat)'s
feelings were not hurt because Louise did not want him.

Alfie felt a tiny bit sorry for Louise too. She was so cross and disappointed. Then he quietly made up his mind. He slipped off his chair and went to whisper in Dad's ear.

"Alfie has a suggestion to make," said Dad out loud.

Alfie went over to Louise and said, "I'll swap my bubble bath for your prize if you like."

Louise thought that was an excellent idea.

So they swapped prizes right away.

Now Louise was all smiles.
She said she was going to ask
Alfie to tea at her house next
Saturday and let him have a
go on her new trampoline.

Then they waved
goodbye, Louise
clutching her bubble
bath and Alfie holding
the consolation prize
tightly in his arms.

When the Harvest Fair was over the children who had painted pictures were allowed to take them home. Alfie carried his painting carefully rolled under one arm and his consolation prize under the other.

On the way out they met Bernard, looking very pleased with himself.

"My beetle has won a prize for being the smallest pet," he told Alfie. "And I got a packet of chocolate buttons."

Alfie and Annie Rose looked into the jam jar. But they still could not see Bernard's prize-winning beetle, only leaves.

"He's had a very exciting day," said Bernard. "He may be feeling a bit tired."

Then he gave Alfie and Annie Rose two chocolate buttons each.

As soon as they got home Annie Rose wanted to do a painting of her own. Luckily there was plenty of paint left in the palette. When she had finished she made Mum stick her picture up on the fridge too, underneath Alfie's.

Alfie sat his prize on the windowsill next to his old knitted elephant, Flumbo.

"What will you call him?" Dad wanted to know.

Alfie thought for a while. He was remembering a name he had often seen on a bus which passed near their street, which he had asked Mum to spell out for him. He liked the sound of it.

"His name is Willesden," he told them all.

"I think that suits him very well," said Mum.

And that is how Willesden stopped being a consolation prize and became part of the family.

Things to do in October

Harvest

In the Harvest Festival people give thanks for the crops that have grown during the past season. If there is a Harvest Fair near you, it might be fun to take part. You could grow your own fruit and vegetables or enter a painting competition like Alfie in *Alfie Wins a Prize*. Why don't you have a painting competition with your friends? Who will be the judge? Will there be a prize?

Leaves

As the autumn leaves change colour and fall from the trees, you can create beautiful pictures. Collect a variety of leaves – all different shapes and sizes. Draw round them to make bold patterns. You can create rubbings by placing the leaf on a firm surface with the veins facing upwards. Put a sheet of white paper on top and, with a soft crayon, rub lightly backwards and forwards over the paper. You could also have a go at bark rubbing. Hold some paper against a tree trunk and rub a soft crayon across it. It's usually possible to identify a tree just by the pattern of its bark!

Potato printing

Autumn is also the perfect time to try potato printing. You will need to ask a grown-up to help you cut a potato in half. On the inside of one half draw a shape for your print. Ask your adult helper to score along the outline of your drawing and cut away the surrounding potato. Then you can paint your cut potato shape and stamp the design onto paper. You can make lots of different shapes and use different bright colours to make greetings cards and wrapping paper.

Writing letters

You can use decorated cards and pieces of paper to write your own letters. Enclose something small and light like a photograph, some paper dolls or a pressed flower, and ask an adult to help you find the right stamps when you go to the post office. You can write to a friend, a relative, or you can even find a pen friend. It's nice to write letters to people, but even more exciting to receive one back!

If you want to write a secret message to someone, you can write it backwards like this:

Meet me at the pond. *(mirror-writing)*

To read the message, all your pen friend has to do is hold it up to a mirror. Mirror-writing takes a bit of practice, so use a pencil and eraser before you go over the writing in ink.

Halloween

October is also the month of Halloween. On the 31st, people dress up in scary costumes and have parties with their friends. A favourite game is Apple Bobbing: each player tries to grab an apple floating in a bucket of water between their teeth – the size of the apple is supposed to show the size of your fortune!

Halloween costumes

There are lots of things around the house that you can use to make a costume for Halloween. You can stuff an old pair of tights to make a cat's tail, or stuff four pairs to make eight spider's legs and ask an adult to help you sew them onto an old T-shirt. A large piece of black card can make a brilliant witch's hat. You will need to

draw a curve from the corner of the card to the longest edge, and then ask an adult to cut along this line. Roll the circle round on itself to make a cone shape, and get the adult to fit it on your head and tape it together. To make the brim of your witch's hat, stand the cone on a second piece of black card and draw around it. Draw a larger circle around this so that you have a ring shape. Ask the adult to cut this out and then make small snips around the base of your cone. Fold the snipped edges outwards, dab some glue on these tabs, place the ring over the cone and press firmly in place. You can have fun decorating the witch's hat with spider webs and stars.

Old Man's Beard

In autumn, Old Man's Beard (which in summertime is known as Wild Clematis or Traveller's Joy) loses its flowers, and can be seen rambling through hedgerows and trees along the roadside with a tangle of climbing shoots and a mass of silvery seed heads.

November

This is the season of burning leaves, bonfires and fireworks shooting up into the night sky, leaving behind a trail of dazzling coloured lights. It's often the month of Diwali, and now that the evenings are dark early and it's chilly outside, it's a good time for indoor games.

Some birds have flown away to warmer places, and animals like hedgehogs and dormice need to find somewhere to curl up and sleep until the spring comes again.

Late Song

We glimpsed an old man in the late afternoon
(Rustling, shuffling, dry leaves scuffling)
In fading light with a sliver of moon
And the sun just going down.

He tramped past the wood by the side of the hill
(Nuts and berries, dark like cherries)
And where he walked it was suddenly chill
And the golden leaves turned brown.

And a brisk wind whipped through the shivering grass
(Sighing, moaning, branches groaning)
And stirred his beard as we saw him pass,
So nimble and yet so old.

But as his shadow was growing long
(Lean and lank in the chilly dank)
A robin whistled a last brave song
To herald the coming cold.

The Very Special Birthday

Alfie had plenty of friends at nursery school, but his best friend was Bernard. They often played together after school. Bernard had a huge collection of cars and trucks and aeroplanes. When Alfie came to play at his house, they got them all out and raced them across the floor.

Bernard didn't have a special cuddly toy that he liked as much as Alfie liked his dear old knitted elephant, Flumbo. Usually Bernard took his favourite racing car to bed with him.

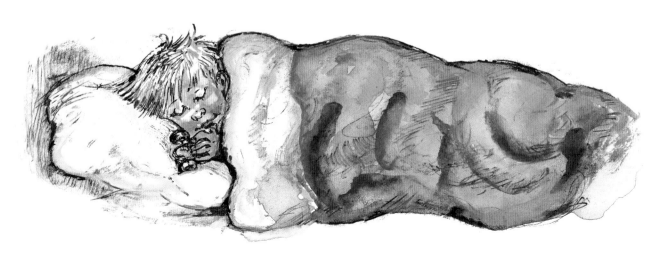

For his birthday, Alfie had given Bernard a book full of pictures of aeroplanes, which he liked a lot. He knew the names of most of them, even the old-fashioned ones. He had seen them in a museum.

One day Bernard came to play at Alfie's house and he brought his aeroplane book with him. After they had looked at it for a while, Mum asked them if they would like to help her ice a cake for another very special birthday. It was for Alfie's Great-Grandma Hilary.

Mum told them that she was ninety years old today, and that was very old indeed.

Alfie and Bernard helped Mum to spread the chocolate icing on the cake and make it smooth. Then they put nine candles on it (one for every ten years), and wrote a big "90" in the middle in tiny jelly sweets.

Mum said that after lunch they were going to drive to the home where Great-Grandma Hilary lived with some other elderly ladies and gentlemen, and she asked Bernard if he would like to come too.

Alfie did not think that this sounded like a very interesting plan. He thought it would be much nicer to stay at home and play with Bernard. But Bernard thought it was an excellent idea. He had never met a great-grandma before and he wanted to see what she looked like. He imagined she would be very big, perhaps even a giant.

So while Mum was wrapping up Great-Grandma Hilary's present of a beautiful silk scarf, Alfie and Bernard made birthday cards for her. Alfie drew a cake on his and put a big "90" on it in coloured dots. Bernard drew a huge lady with two tiny people standing next to her, who were himself and Alfie.

After lunch, Mum put Great-Grandma Hilary's cake and present and a bunch of flowers into the car, along with Annie Rose, and they all set out. Bernard brought his aeroplane book and Alfie took Flumbo.

When they arrived, they were shown into a room where
everyone was sitting, and there was Great-Grandma Hilary
in a big armchair. Bernard was very surprised when he saw
her, because she was not huge at all! She was a very small lady.
But she smiled a big smile when she saw them.

She was very pleased with all the things they had brought, especially Alfie and Bernard's cards.

When the candles on the cake were lit and everyone in the room had sung "Happy Birthday", Great-Grandma Hilary asked Bernard and Alfie if they would help her blow them out. She thought she might not have enough puff to do it on her own.

After tea, she gave Alfie the beautiful silver ribbon which Mum had used to tie up her present and helped him to make a bow around Flumbo's neck. Then she asked Bernard if he would kindly show her his aeroplane book. Bernard was even more surprised when they went through it together and she knew the names of all the old-fashioned planes.

She told Bernard that when she was young she had worked in a factory where they had actually made aeroplanes. She knew a lot about what kind of engines they had. And once she had been to an airfield and seen the pilots take off and do stunts in the sky, looping the loop and diving over the control tower.

When it was time to say goodbye, Mum and Alfie and Annie Rose gave Great-Grandma Hilary a big hug. Then it was Alfie's turn to be surprised, because Bernard gave Great-Grandma Hilary a big hug too. And hugging people was something that Bernard did not often do.

When they got back home, Alfie and Bernard both ran about with their arms spread wide, making loud aeroplane noises. They ran all over the living room and the hall, and down the passage and around the kitchen table, until at last they were so tired that they made a crash landing on the floor. It had been a very special day.

Things to do in November

Fireworks

The Hindu festival of Diwali is often celebrated with colourful fireworks. In Great Britain, people "remember, remember the fifth of November", and light bonfires, fireworks and sparklers. You can make your own beautiful firework pictures by covering some white card with a layer of different-coloured bright crayons. Now add a layer of black crayon on top. Then, using a lollipop stick or a key, scrape off some of the black crayon in firework shapes to reveal the colours beneath. Be careful not to press too hard or you will scrape off the coloured layer too.

Holding a party

In *The Very Special Birthday* Alfie visits his great-grandma Hilary. November is a great month for visiting friends and family; as the evenings are dark and it's cold outside, it's a good time for cosy indoor activities.

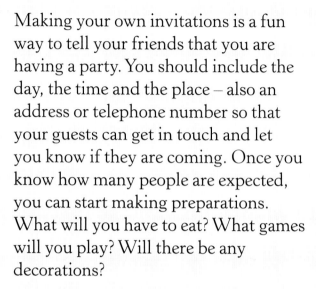

Making your own invitations is a fun way to tell your friends that you are having a party. You should include the day, the time and the place – also an address or telephone number so that your guests can get in touch and let you know if they are coming. Once you know how many people are expected, you can start making preparations. What will you have to eat? What games will you play? Will there be any decorations?

Bunting

Bunting is easy to make yourself. Ask an adult to help you cut out triangles of paper and then paint them, colour them in or perhaps write a message that goes across several triangles. Make a hole in two of the corners (but not right at the point) of each triangle and thread string through the holes. Now you'll have a beautiful string of bunting to hang from the ceiling!

Party games

There are lots of fun party games you can play indoors with your friends:

Sardines

This is a game for small groups. You will need somewhere with hiding spaces that are big enough for a few people.

First choose who will be "it". This player goes to hide while the others count to 20. Once they have finished counting, everyone tries to find "it"; any player who finds the hider joins them in their hiding place until there is only one player left not hiding. Now it's their turn to hide.

Musical bumps

Lots of players can join in this game. You just need a space to dance in, and some music. Everyone must dance around to the music, but when it stops, they must quickly sit on the floor. The last player to sit down is out, and should go and sit at the side. The winner is the last player left in. Musical statues is a similar game, but when the music stops, all players must freeze in their position. If a player is caught moving before the music starts again, they are out.

Squeak Piggy Squeak

One player is chosen to be blindfolded and is placed in the middle of the other seated players. This player is spun around a few times until dizzy, and then finds a lap to sit on, saying *"Squeak Piggy Squeak"*, at which point the person underneath lets out a squeak and the blindfolded player has to guess who it is.

Pass the Parcel

This needs to be prepared before your guests arrive. You should wrap the prize in lots of layers of wrapping paper, placing smaller prizes – perhaps sweets or small toys – in between random layers. The players sit in a circle and pass the parcel around while the music plays. When it stops, the player left holding the parcel can unwrap one layer of paper. When the music starts again, players continue passing the parcel, until a player unwraps the last layer and wins the prize.

Holly

Christmas decorations are often made
from the red berries and prickly green
leaves of the holly tree. In winter, blackbirds
gorge themselves on holly berries and spread
the seeds. Many birds will nest in holly
or roost in it in winter, as its spiky leaves
protect them from predators.

December

Christmas is coming! Will it be white with snow? There's so much to do: shopping, presents to wrap, the Christmas tree to decorate.

This is the season of cooking and carol singing, holly and mistletoe. Will you try to make an Advent Calendar? Or some paper chains? Or some delicious biscuits to hand round when the family get together on Christmas Day?

This is the time of the birth of Jesus, of comfort and joy and peace on earth. Happy Christmas, everyone!

A Midwinter Night's Dream

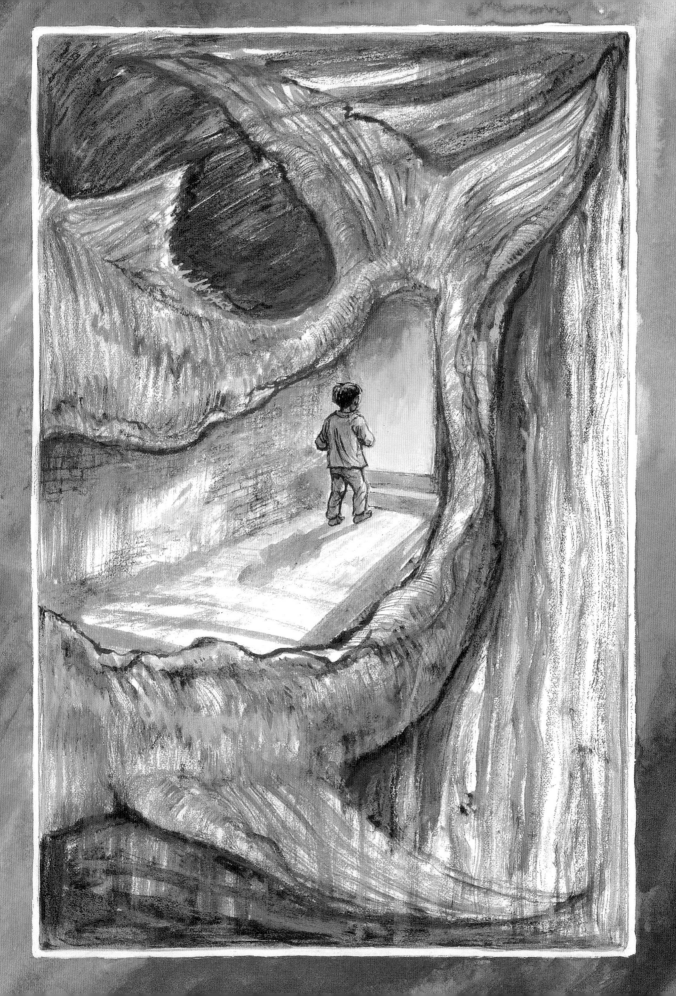

One Winter Evening

One winter evening, time for bed,
One winter evening late,
We heard a bird with a breast of red
Sing by the garden gate.

He cocked his head with its bright black eye
And sang in the still damp air,
And a star came out in a pale yellow sky
And silently twinkled there.

Goose Weather

Snow!
White flakes, floating and falling,
Blotting out windows,
Covering rooftops and cars and gardens,
Feathery light.
Somewhere up there,
Above the over-stuffed clouds,
Muffled in mist,
The Snow Goose is taking flight.

Things to do in December

December marks the start of the festive season; it's time to begin the preparations for Christmas. It's cold and icy outside, and there might even be snow. In *Goose Weather*, the snow goose takes flight over the snow-covered rooftops. Here is a traditional Christmas carol about a goose: it can be sung in a round:

> *Christmas is coming, the goose is*
> *   getting fat,*
> *Please put a penny in the old man's*
> *   hat,*
> *If you haven't got a penny, then a*
> *   ha'penny will do,*
> *If you haven't got a ha'penny, then*
> *   God bless you!*

Games in the snow

These are some activities that you can try outside in the snow, making sure of course that you keep warm and dry:

- Of course, you can build a snowman by rolling a large ball of snow for the body and a smaller one for the head. Use a carrot for the nose and pieces of coal or pebbles for the eyes, mouth and buttons. Add some sticks for the arms. Top off with a hat and tie a woolly scarf around its neck.

- To make a snow angel, lie down on a clear patch of snow with your arms and legs outstretched. Move your arms and legs up and down across the snow, keeping them straight, and then carefully stand up to admire your angel.

- If you have plenty of snow, then you can make an igloo or a snow den. Once you have made the den out of snow bricks, you can pour water over it at night so the walls freeze hard and solid.

Winter crafts and games

At Christmas people tend to decorate their houses with lights and colourful decorations. Paper chains look very festive and can easily be made using scrap paper. Ask an adult to help you cut strips of paper: they need to be the same length and width – the more colourful the better. Using glue, tape or staples, stick the ends of the first strip together to form a loop. Place the second strip through the loop and stick together. Keep doing this until you have a colourful chain to hang from the walls or ceiling.

Hanukkah, the Jewish Festival of Lights, is also often celebrated in December: one candle in a special candelabrum is lit each day. Games are often played during Hanukkah; the most common uses a four-sided wooden spinning top called a dreidel.

Families gather together at Christmas and Hanukkah, and people often give each other presents. Is there anything you can make to give to your friends and family? Baking cakes or biscuits is a nice idea; and you can make your own festive cards to send.

Time capsule
The end of the year is a great time to make a time capsule. Choose a container that is strong, watertight and big enough to hold the objects you want to bury. Pick items that show what you have done this year: they can be photographs, tickets, objects – anything that is a special memory for you. Write a letter to go in the box, and remember to include the date, details of who you are and any special message you want to leave. Bury your time capsule (if there's nowhere you can bury it, then why not hide it in your house instead – in the attic or a cupboard). Who will find your time capsule? And what will have changed by the time they find it? Or you can set a date for one, two or even five years in the future to open your own time capsule and look back and remember all the special things you did that year.

* * *

Now the year has come to an end – but there's a new one just around the corner! We all start again in January, and who knows what this year will bring?

Have a very happy new year with lots of stories to share and new things to do . . .

with love from
Shirley Hughes x

Some other books by Shirley Hughes:

ALFIE GETS IN FIRST
ALFIE GIVES A HAND
AN EVENING AT ALFIE'S
ALFIE AND THE BIRTHDAY SURPRISE
ALFIE AND THE BIG BOYS
ALFIE'S CHRISTMAS
ALFIE'S ALPHABET
ALFIE'S NUMBERS
THE BIG ALFIE AND ANNIE ROSE STORYBOOK
ANNIE ROSE IS MY LITTLE SISTER
THE ALFIE TREASURY
DOGGER
SALLY'S SECRET
UP AND UP
ABEL'S MOON
MOVING MOLLY
THE LION AND THE UNICORN
THE SHIRLEY HUGHES COLLECTION
A LIFE DRAWING
A BRUSH WITH THE PAST